BONES OF CONNECTION

BONNIE ELIZABETH

My Big Fat Orange Cat Publishing

Chapter One

If I had known what taking the job on Jewel Island would have gotten me into, I might have stayed in my sister's basement. As a forty-three-year-old divorced, fat woman I didn't exactly have my pick of jobs. Jewel had felt like my last hope. But a line has to be drawn even at last hopes.

The day I left for the interview, I had my sister drop me at the ferry terminal. The bright sunny day had boded well. Jewel wasn't an island I could find on a map, which was weird. A ticket to the ferry had been left for me, and despite my misgivings, I figured the worst that would happen was I had to buy a ticket back from Milwaukee when the ferry landed across the lake, even if the creepy guy who sat in on the interview glowering at me was there in person.

I hung out on the top deck, enjoying the blue sky and the cool breeze. A few young girls laughed and giggled when I moved my chair slightly away so that I could sit, my heavy hips and thighs hanging over the edge. I set my overnight bag at my feet and pulled my arms through my sweater, despite the sun.

Just as I was starting to relax, the girls' giggles subsiding into conversations about other things and no longer making me uncomfortable, fog started to come up. I've been in heavy fog. I've watched the days change quickly, but never this quickly. Perhaps it wasn't unusual for a lake but I didn't live on Lake Michigan, although it was an easy drive from my home town.

The girls and the other passengers all headed inside, leaving me alone out there, smelling the soggy odor of garbage and gasoline that permeated the fog. It felt as bad as it smelled.

Fortunately, the ferry slowed sooner than I expected, the baritone honking of the horn warning all in its path where it was. I hoped this was the island, though as it slowed more, I wasn't so sure. I couldn't see much of anything, although I had gotten up and moved to the rail. The fog was so thick I could barely see my hand in front of my face.

The stink of dead fish rising up around me was enough to put me off seafood for the rest of my life. I began to wonder if this job was for me, no matter how desperate I might be. I'd been so thrilled to finally get an in-person interview and at a job that might actually pay decently. If putting up with the stink was part of the job, no wonder they had to pay so well.

An older woman and an emaciated man had interviewed me online. She'd called herself the mayor of Jewel Island. When they'd offered me an in-person interview, I'd accepted, which led to the tickets and ferry ride.

The eerie feeling I'd had when I hadn't been able to find the island on the map returned. A small island between Michigan and Wisconsin, right on the ferry run should have been a major place for tourists. Instead, it was as if the island didn't exist. Even Google earth images of

Lake Michigan showed no island in the vicinity of where it must be based on the information I had.

Once again, I pushed away my unease. I could handle this. It was only an overnight. My sisters knew where I was, though they, too, had concerns about not finding the island. If I were lost, my sisters would help. We'd keep in touch by cell phone and my youngest sister had put an app on mine to let her know where I was, just in case.

We'd laughed about it because last year on my birthday they'd taken me axe throwing. I'd been surprisingly good, the best of all of us when I'd done it. There was just the small matter of finding an axe if I needed one. After we'd laughed, she'd showed me the app and how it worked so that if I wanted to turn it off, I could.

I might not have a husband and children, but I had sisters who loved me. I wasn't alone in the world, nor was I destitute, thanks to Charlene letting me live in her basement.

Unsurprisingly, I was the only one to get off. At least the giggling girls weren't following me down the gang plank. I appreciated the warmth of my heavy sweater but could have wished for a light jacket to keep the dampness from my skin. I usually appreciate the insulation my fat gives me in Michigan winters, but even I'm not impervious to damp. Chances were, the soft yarn of my sweater was picking up the dead fish stink and I'd smell through my interview, though that wasn't until the next day.

I sighed. I turned around, as if the fog would let me see the ferry, perhaps raise a hand to flag it back down to return and get me, but I was buried in the cloud bank along with the rest of the island. Maybe the island would look better not framed in gray and dampness.

The sound of the ferry chugging through the waters receded and I was left with the sound of the small waves lapping against the rocky beach on this side of the island. I breathed out, trying to calm myself.

Someone had built a parking lot, albeit one designed for about four cars. A bleached wood shack sat in one corner. I could almost make out a blue design on the side. Probably a fish. I walked closer. The shack was shuttered and closed, but it suggested that someone might run the place.

I shouldered the overnight bag and walked towards what ought to be the road. As I moved, the fog seemed to lift. The road became clearer, a concrete path wide enough for a single car. To my left the road appeared flat for the short distance I could see. Small scrub trees lined it on one side. Rocks lined the lake side, except for a few hardy stragglers holding on for dear life between the boulders.

Two parts of the road headed to the right, one making a hard right, following the beach but angling up a hill, another angling down behind the hill into what might be a valley, although I couldn't begin to tell for certain, given the fog.

From the direction of the hill, I heard a sudden blast of music that was cut off as quickly as it had come, rather as if a door had opened and then closed. At least the music indicated people. It'd been too short a burst for me to catch the tune, but the intuitive part of my brain said it sounded modern.

That small comfort had all the warmth of the fog that wrapped around me. I'd read enough spooky stories about someone lost and finding a ghost town, being wined and dined only to wake up and find themselves in a shack. The island had that feel to it.

I stepped out onto the concrete after looking both ways. I didn't hear any cars and hopefully one wouldn't come silently racing around a corner I didn't know about and hit me as I tried to get my bearings.

There were buildings both up the hill and on the angled road that curved deeper into the island. Lights shone from a low building along the straighter path. I wanted to head that way, but something prodded me to walk up the hill.

Sharon, the woman who had interviewed me, said that they'd put me up at the Jewel B&B.

"It's the only place on the island, really, unless you have family here," she'd said happily.

I said I didn't.

Sharon had replied she knew. Damien, the man with her had almost glowered as if he hated being on the call.

Sharon was bright and warm, her hair gray, her face lined. She was heavy enough to look like a grandmother that baked and cooked and gave hugs that would take away even the worst of hurts. In fact, I had sort of longed to hug her.

The man, though…he could have starred in just about any horror movie he wanted, though I'd have pegged him for a vampire. Or at the very least a serial killer. Dark hair, a long narrow face, and a mouth with corners that naturally turned down, he looked imposing enough. Worse, he had the palest skin I'd ever seen. I'd been able to see blue veins beneath it when he leaned forward to adjust something on his computer with fingers spiderlike in their thinness.

With a name like Damien Bain he'd have no problems getting the part even if he didn't look like such a stereotypical monster.

Damien had let Sharon talk. He'd sat and watched, as still as a corpse, which, if he were a vampire, he'd be. His face had just enough lines for me to believe he was older than his dark hair suggested and I had wondered if he dyed it to look younger.

If he'd been the one interviewing me, no matter the job title and salary, I'd have told them I couldn't possibly live on an island and hope that my sister Charlene didn't kill me for not accepting the job. She did want her basement back but not at the expense of me dying, or becoming undead if Damien were actually a vampire.

I continued to listen for a car and then turned and started up the hill. The fog seemed to be even thinner, now. In fact, I noted traces of blue sky above me, though the fog still softened the edges of the day.

The buildings around me were mostly wood, though some had brick façades. A larger building with plenty of brown paper taped over the windows highlighting sales—apples were on sale that week—Don't miss out!—had a single glass door leading inside. Lights flooded out onto the gray street. A grocery store, though it wasn't all that much larger than a convenience store.

Across the way I saw a shop that said clothing. It looked like a little gray house. The angle of the hill made it look like it was leaning ever so slightly to the side.

I was immediately taken back to the nightmare story of the woman stuck in a ghost town, waking to find herself in a shack. With Damien around, perhaps I'd never wake up, or if I did, I'd be a vampire.

Maybe as a vampire, I'd be thin.

I'd never been thin in my life and I often felt ashamed of my body. I worked towards body positivity. I wanted to love myself as I was. I mean, it wasn't like I hadn't dieted all my life, trying to fit in, but apparently, that wasn't to be. I wore a size 28 or sometimes a 26. Even if the little island clothing store had clothing, I doubted anything would fit me.

I sighed and continued up the hill. Rich and savory smells came from a narrow door labeled just "Derry's." It might have been a restaurant but the building was hardly wider than the glass door which looked almost too narrow to admit me. They wouldn't be feeding many people if I couldn't even get inside. Even thin people needed a bit of space to eat.

The hill was steep, but I walked a lot. I liked going out for nature walks. Other people might call them hikes, but living in Michigan, I thought of them as walks. When I'd been younger and fully employed and married, I'd traveled out to the west coast and did some real hikes on trails up the lower portion of real mountains.

But all that was in the past. My ex-husband's family owned the company that I'd done the accounting for and when he'd left me, he'd suggested it would be best for everyone if I didn't work there any longer. I'd gotten a good severance package and a decent amount from the sale of the house we'd shared for nearly twenty years, but a forty-three year old fat woman had two strikes against her in the job world as soon as she showed up, no matter what her experience was.

I'd been relegated to applying for bookkeeping positions and even those didn't want me despite being overqualified. I'd get the first interview, the employer would see me, and then decide to "go another way." This was one of the rare second interviews and it was for the position of accountant. Sharon had been so nice that I had my fingers crossed for this one even if the job did include living on an island with a vampirish man named Damien Bain.

On the side of the street that overlooked the lake, I noticed the sign for Jewel Accounting and Bookkeeping on a building that looked a bit like a remodeled house. Long and low, with only a narrow front porch to break up the line, it sat back from the street, the front area all concrete as if it were a parking lot waiting for the cars I had yet to see.

The building was gray and looked sturdier than some of the buildings further down the hill, or maybe it was the perspective. Instead of looking up at it and seeing it at an angle, I was across the street.

I had yet to see any people wandering around. Outside of the blast of music, I hadn't heard anything either. I could have been alone on the entire island. Despite the fog having thinned even further and the blue sky brightening overhead, the feeling of being alone sent a chill down my spine.

I continued up the hill, hoping for something that looked like a B&B. On the left side, away from the lake was a large Victorian house painted pink and green, the brightest colors I'd seen since I left the ferry. A small wood sign outside held the words bed and breakfast. Nothing else. In a car, driving by, even at a mere fifteen miles an hour, the words would have been easy to miss.

The Victorian had no parking area, unlike some of the other buildings. Instead, it had an overflowing garden with a narrow walk to the door. Though many of the plants were beginning their dormancy—the calendar showing early October—there were plenty of green leaves and a few hardier flowers of sorts that I couldn't name. Gardening had never been an interest of mine.

A small tree, less twisted and scraggly than the ones I'd seen upon arriving stood to one side of the walk. Even so it remained bent over with its branches reaching out towards the building like an old woman reaching for help to stand up.

I passed it as I went up the walk, noticing three cats, one black, one orange striped, and one pure white, sitting beneath the tree. I paused and squatted down. They were the first living things I'd seen since leaving the ferry. The relief I felt was more pronounced than I would have expected.

I held out my hand and the golden-eyed black cat stood up and stretched, staring at me. The others didn't move. I might have been a ghost, or perhaps a human in a ghost world, though I could easily see the rise and fall of the feline's chests and the movement of their eyes.

I sighed and stood up.

As I did so, I nearly jumped a foot backwards, I was so startled to see Sharon standing on the porch of the Victorian as if she'd been there all along.

Chapter Two

A moment ago, I'd noticed the porch, white paint against the pink and green, huddled next to the rounded turret area on the left. I'd been heading for the three steps that led from the front garden when I'd noticed the cats. No one had been standing there. A white bench sat next to the building with more plants but unless Sharon had been squatting down, hiding from me, I couldn't have missed her.

"You've found us," Sharon said. She was solidly built, with little waist definition. Although she wore jeans, they were loose and her legs wide enough to make the jeans appear to be a skirt. She wore a cream turtleneck with rabbits on the collar under a heavier black wool sweater.

"I thought there would be some direction from the ferry," I said quietly. I wasn't really expecting to talk with someone right then. I'd been told I could freshen up after I was led to the B&B.

Sharon smiled. "If you weren't right for the position, you'd never have found the place."

I had an image of myself wandering around the island,

trying to find a place to stay, not succeeding and dying, alone in an unknown and unexplored place. An involuntary shudder ran down my back. The image and the sensation were so clear, my mouth dried.

Sharon shook her head, almost as if reading my mind. "That's not what would have happened at all. You'd have wandered around, decided this was wrong for you, and found that the ferry had come back to pick you up."

I frowned, worried that she actually did read minds and I hoped I'd not been unflattering in my assessment of her. At least I'd liked her so that was less likely. If it were Damien there, I'd have been in trouble.

"I'm not a mind reader," Sharon said. "I don't think any of us are. But everyone has that fear when they arrive and learn that they would only get to stay if they find the B&B."

I wondered who everyone was. If others had applied and interviewed for the accounting position and turned it down, there could be problems I didn't know about, and not just Sharon's mysterious comments about finding the B&B.

"But come on in and let's get you settled." Sharon gestured to me. The cats were now settled under the tree ignoring me, even the black one.

I picked up my carry-on bag and walked up the three steps. Sharon watched me closely.

It felt odd having her watch me, almost as if she wasn't sure I could make it. I might have been fat, but I was able-bodied. People so often underestimated me. It's not that not being abled was a problem, it was the assumption that I couldn't be fat and still be perfectly fit and healthy that annoyed me.

The double front doors were painted green with oval

glass insets and were quite pretty. Sharon opened the right-side door and gestured me inside.

Once inside, I took in the golden-brown, thin-board hardwood floors and the matching woodwork on the lower half of the walls. A stairwell led upstairs just beyond a sitting room on my right. To my left a door opened into the room that held the rounded front. It was devoid of people but small tables were scattered around. A dining room.

Ahead of me was a small writing table, of the sort popular in Victorian times, naturally. It blended well with the cream, green, and purple floral wallpaper that lined the upper part of the walls. Like the garden outside, it was all a bit much. The place pushed the visual senses to over-flowing. A calico cat peeked out from under the table, eyeing me with great golden eyes.

A young man sashayed out of the dining area.

"Are you Holly?" he asked, smiling at me. He was thin and very blonde, his heart-shaped face almost pretty in the way girls were supposed to be pretty, but often weren't. He wore a white button-down shirt under a red and black plaid flannel vest with black jeans and red high-tops. One ear was pierced.

"I am," I said.

"I'm Ian. Sharon has you registered, so I'll just take you to your room. We have one back here for you. It doesn't have a view of the lake, but it's a comfortable room, if that's okay?" he asked.

I nodded.

He led me past the writing desk to a small alcove behind the sitting room in front. A door in the same shiny golden-brown as the floors greeted us. A blackened brass number 3 adorned it at my eye-level.

Surprisingly, it held a modern lock and Ian gave me a keycard of the sort you find in chain hotels. I only had to hold it in front of the mechanism and the door would unlock.

I must have raised an eyebrow because Ian laughed.

"I know. You'd think we'd stick to old-fashioned keys but the B&B likes to keep up with technology."

I had a vision of the old house sitting in front of a giant laptop reading up on technology and carefully making decisions about what to use and not use. Ian's use of language was odd. He sashayed back to wherever he came from after opening the door for me, not even waiting to see if the room was acceptable, although I had to admit, he'd done more than most hoteliers would have done.

I stepped into a room that really did overwhelm the senses. A Persian style rug in green and cream covered the floor nearest the bed. The wallpaper continued in another print and a colorful green, cream, and purple quilt lay across the bed. A large chest of drawers sat against the wall next to the door and an embroidered seat sat in front of a vanity or desk, depending on the needs of the guest, which sat against the other wall. In a far corner, over in front of a door that no doubt went to a bathroom, sat two chairs upholstered in a lavender fabric covered in large flowers.

If the rest of the B&B overflowed with sensory stimulation, this one drowned a guest in it. I'd be closing my eyes quickly to avoid becoming ill with all the competing patterns and prints.

"Let's have a seat," Sharon said, pushing me inside.

I hadn't realized she'd followed me.

I wanted to say something about needing to freshen up. The ferry ride hadn't been that long and I was dressed decently, but not perfectly. I'd expected time to comb my hair at the least. But she was here, not just someone showing me to the B&B, but someone to tell me what was going happen.

Sharon took the chair with the back to the bathroom. The door was open and I noted plain white subway tile in there. I almost said a prayer of thanks. I could hide there when the army of prints threatened to overrun my senses.

As I sat in the lavender chair, I noted that I smelled the scent of its namesake herb. A table between the two chairs had a little ceramic (hand-painted with a floral print, of course) dish of potpourri. A large window looked out at a wood fence painted with, of all things, sunflowers. Just in case the room didn't have enough color.

The heat clicked on with a hum and groan and warm air breathed down on me in the chair. I hadn't thought I felt cold, but I appreciated the heat. Normally, I'm always hot, but the fog had brought with it a damp chill that was hard to shake.

"I know you want to freshen up," Sharon said, "and you will before we go to dinner in a short while. At dinner we can talk more about your experiences here and whether or not you want to stay to meet Jack, the bookkeeper you'll be working with if you take the job."

I nodded.

"But first, we need to talk about your magic."

I blinked at her. "Excuse me?"

"Your magic."

I blinked again. I thought she said magic. Like I had any.

"I'm sorry?"

Sharon gave me that smile again, one that should have calmed me but now felt a bit patronizing. No wonder they couldn't keep an accountant. She was crazy and Damien looked like a vampire. People probably arrived and ran screaming back to the ferry.

"Only someone with magic could have followed our instructions to get here. The final test was the walk up the hill. It's not obvious that this is the way to go. The police station has those lights and the fog means that people naturally want to head that way. It started lifting even as you decided to go up the hill, didn't it?" Sharon said.

I frowned. The timing was about right.

"What did you see on the way up?"

"The grocery store. A clothing store. Several other places. A restaurant that looked too narrow to have any tables. The B&B."

"And heard?"

"Mostly the waves lapping at the island. There was a brief bit of music but it stopped like someone had opened and closed a door," I said.

Sharon nodded, bringing her hands together softly in a silent clap.

She dug around in a purse that I hadn't noticed before. She brought out several tea candles in their own little metal tins.

"Light the candle," she said.

"I didn't bring any matches," I replied.

Sharon shook her head. She was still smiling, but this was that of a teacher with a particularly slow student.

Then, instead of telling me to do it, she half-closed her eyes and stared at the candle. My arms began to tingle. Moments later the candle was lit.

I drew back, fascinated. Having a moment to think about the candle being lit, I realized this could have been staged. A magician's trick. Wasn't that how people got drawn into things like this? Not that I had heard of people on an island that wasn't supposed to exist drawing people to them to kill them or perhaps take their fortune, which, sadly, I did not have.

"Now you try," Sharon said. She was watching me.

I half-closed my eyes and thought about fire. I didn't

expect to light the candle, but I did expect that whatever trick had manifested itself with Sharon would work for me, too. I just had to pretend and she'd be thrilled that I could light the candle and offer me all sorts of teachings because I was, apparently, special.

I knew better.

Magic didn't exist.

Nothing happened. If Sharon was playing me, she was good. Or she was particularly adept at reading people.

"Accountants." She twisted her mouth at the statement as if it were a bad thing. "I always prefer creative types. They're so much more willing to give themselves to the magic, to believe it's real."

"Is that what this is about? Some cult believing in magic?" I asked. If it was, there was no way I could work there. No matter how good of a job, how much they paid. Charlene would understand why I remained in her basement.

I worked off my rent by taking care of the kids, driving them places and contributing to the kitchen larder. I could whine about never having children of my own, and often enough I did, because my ex now had a child, just not with me, or I could enjoy my nieces and nephews. Charlene had four kids and even before I'd been unemployed I'd been pulled in to babysit.

Now the kids were all older and we could play games. They weren't quite old enough to be completely left alone and young teenagers presented their own logistical problems. Having me living in the basement solved both of them. Charlene or her husband, Aaron, hadn't had to go out and get a babysitter the kids would complain about, but they also weren't leaving them to their own devices.

"Not at all," Sharon said. "However, magic requires that you put some effort into it."

She waved a hand over the lit candle and half-closed her eyes. Once again, I felt the tingling in my arms. It came on slower this time. I almost felt some sort of energy in the room rising up and surrounding me until the candle flame lit and then it stopped.

"Did you feel that?" she asked.

I nodded. Trick or not, I had felt something. Perhaps it was whatever they used to light the candle.

"Try and recreate the sensation in your body," Sharon said.

I frowned. I hadn't felt anything in my body.

She waved away the flame from the lit candle. I thought about the sensations on my arms. Nothing happened.

I kept at it. Far be it from me to say that I gave up. I tried to imagine what the sensations felt like, but imagining didn't bring them on.

"I think you're focusing too much on the external. Let's try this again. I want you to close your eyes and think about how your body feels when I do this."

I wanted to ask how I'd know what she was doing, but decided the tingling on my arms would let me know. I closed my eyes.

In addition to the tingle on my arms that got stronger over the next few seconds, I felt a heat rising up through my body. I wondered if I were feeling wherever they were pulling the flame from. Maybe someone sat beneath the floorboards with some sort of laser and I was feeling that heat up.

Except that sounded just as silly as someone creating a flame via magic, if not more so.

I smelled the burning of a candle flame. My eyes flew open.

"Now, I want you to work on the feeling you just had and light the next candle," Sharon said quietly.

I wasn't sure why, but I closed my eyes again and prepared to focus. If this was a trick it was an elaborate one. I wasn't ready to believe in magic. Not yet. But I would go along with this because if Sharon were willing to put on this charade, who knew what else she'd do. Perhaps I'd have been safer wandering around the island, lost.

Still, I found the warmth down in my lower abdomen and felt it rise up. My arms didn't tingle this time. The warmth rose up and I felt like I tossed it out. I heard a huge whoosh. My eyes snapped open.

The table was on fire, flames burning nearly to the ceiling.

I squealed and pushed the chair away from the burning table. If this was some sort of insurance trick, I'd been had.

Sharon waved a hand and the flames disappeared. "I'd say you have a good amount of power, at least with fire." She smiled at me.

I stared at her.

"Now, can you accept that magic is real?" Sharon asked.

Seeing my face and not getting an immediate yes, she continued, "Or at least accept that it might be real?"

I was able to accept the latter. I still wasn't certain, but whatever they were doing was so elaborate it might have been magic, if it wasn't exactly magic in the way I had been trained to think of it.

"The island is one of many places that attracts people when they start coming into their magic. We're a safe place to learn how to use it and to keep it hidden," Sharon said.

"But you put employment ads online," I said.

"We can spell them so that only people who have some

level of magical ability can see them," Sharon said. "Other people find us just because they turn up on our shores, having been drawn here, though that happens more to places that aren't on islands."

"So, it's not just this island," I repeated.

"No. There are small enclaves all over the world. We call ourselves mages. Witches used to be okay, but the Wiccans started taking back their name, and we decided to go with mages to differentiate ourselves. Wiccans are spiritual beings and there's no requirement to be spiritual to use magic, at least not our magic."

I nodded, thinking maybe I'd gone crazy to even be entertaining these ideas. If I could be certain the ferry would be at the dock or would be there soon, I'd grab my bag and leave. My eyes found the table, noting that it was barely blackened, though the candles on top were just metal cups of melted wax.

"Magic always comes from our most vulnerable place —that place that houses the thing we've been shamed for, the thing that we want to hide from the world," Sharon said. "It might be an action one took as one was young. It might be our body or our sexuality."

I immediately flashed on all the things I was ashamed of. My divorce, which, because my husband had left me and not the other way around, left me ashamed. My lack of a child, because I'd always listened to my husband that we'd start a family soon and yet we never had, though he'd hurried and started a family with another woman. My lack of employment, though that, too, had been tied to my husband and not my job performance. Even my body size was a source of shame, though I was working on accepting that.

"I don't want to know your greatest shame," Sharon said. "For many people it's not even possible to talk about it. But realize that those dark secrets we keep to ourselves, or try to, offer us power. The more accepting of those parts you can be, the more magical power you'll have."

I still wasn't quite ready to embrace the whole magic thing but it was an interesting take.

"Let's head over for dinner. Derry's is wonderful," Sharon said, once again smiling.

I stood up, wondering if I was crazy for not having left already, even if it meant calling for help and chartering a boat.

Chapter Three

Sharon led me back out of the B&B. Ian waved from his place in the dining room. He was setting tables.

"They have dinner here but it's usually just small bites. Maybe a quiche or hot sandwiches. Now and then they do a nice pizza," Sharon said. "Most of us just go to Derry's."

"Are there other restaurants?" I asked. I hadn't seen apartments and had no idea how well appointed the kitchens were.

"No. It's not a big place. We have a deli in the grocery store at the bottom of the hill and people often use that for lunch. Or we cook for ourselves. Small town life and on an island, we don't have the amenities of a city." Sharon sounded almost sad.

The street looked different in the long shadows. There weren't many lights along the road. I still didn't see any cars.

"Do people drive here?" I asked.

"We mostly have golf carts and scooters for the younger set. The island is easier to get around on with those. We even have a repair shop for them. While the place is a bit large to just wander from one end to the other, we can get most places on foot or by golf cart. Our farms mostly have horses, though they do have tractors for the work," Sharon said.

I wondered if golf carts had weight limits.

"We have good internet. I have no idea how because the island isn't on any map. I pay the bill they send us and don't question certain things," Sharon went on.

"Does my cell phone work here?" I thought I'd had bars when I arrived at the dock but couldn't quite remember.

"Of course. We might be small but we do have modern conveniences. Cars are just so big and don't really offer us a lot of advantages," Sharon said. "So we don't have any."

We arrived at the very narrow door. I noted the word "Derry's" printed on the glass. Very old fashioned. I'd expect a bar if it were a wider building.

Sharon went first and stopped at the foot of a steep staircase about four feet from the door. The stairwell was as wide as the building. I frowned. The building hadn't joined any other building on the street.

"Go on up," Sharon said, pressing herself aside. She watched me, as I squeezed myself past her.

I hesitantly put a foot on the first stair. Once again, doubt swooped in. I didn't quite trust that there really was magic. Every rational cell that remained in my body insisted it was a trick. My irritatingly active imagination half expected someone to come down and grab me, throw a bag over my head and carry me out to kill me. Or maybe I just expected a vampire to swoop down and bite me. Nothing happened.

I grabbed the rail and stepped up, aiming for the next step.

My other foot landed on the top landing, having

bypassed the staircase altogether. I stood at the top of the stairs and had to move quickly into the little room at the top so that Sharon could reach me. To my left was a set of glass doors standing open, welcoming. An older man stood at a very dark podium. As he met my eyes, he smiled at me.

Sharon appeared behind me. One moment she wasn't there and the next she was. Turning to me she nodded.

"I needed you to go first, lest you go running out into the street instead of following me up the stairs," she said. Then she patted my hand not unlike the grandmother she reminded me of.

She walked towards the glass doors.

I looked around. The entry area at the top of the stairs looked as narrow as the bottom, but I noticed that an aisle ran next to the stairs up there. An arrow pointed around the wall ahead to the restrooms. The glass doors to the side suggested a wider space, though I had thought the narrow building stood on its own. In fact, I'd been certain of it. The smells of savory meats like steaks or chops reached me. If people could afford to eat at a place like this on the island whenever they went out, the pay scales must be high, otherwise someone would set up a more informal place.

"Hey Bob," Sharon said.

The older man, the maître d, nodded at us. "Is this the accountant?"

"Her name is Holly," Sharon said. The faintest hint of pink rose up around her cheeks as if embarrassed that he didn't know my name.

"Nice to meet you, Holly," Bob said, rather formally. I noted the dark suit and white shirt. He picked up two menus and glanced back from the podium.

Looking over his shoulder, I noted the dark ceiling and

low lights. White table cloths covered each of the tables. A few booths sat next to windows.

"A window seat, I think," Sharon said.

I was about to interject that booths didn't work for me when Bill spoke.

"I have a table at the corner. Would that work?"

I nodded, eagerly. No one ever anticipated the needs of a woman as large as I am. Booths often didn't have tables that moved and tended to squish into my belly. Tables with chairs allowed me to sit as far back as I needed. I noted that the chairs I saw all had arms.

Bob led us across the restaurant. Only a handful of people were eating at that time and all of them perked up at seeing us walk across the room. A new person in a small town. Or perhaps they weren't used to seeing a very fat woman, though I was pleased to note that one of the men looked every bit as large as I was. Of course, he was tall as well.

In the low light, I could see out into the darkness beyond, though it wasn't a great view. During the day, it would be. We were higher than I had expected. I had no idea how the stairs worked or what kind of a trick it was, but clearly it had taken up more than a single flight. Maybe there *was* magic there.

The chairs at our table were armless, unlike the other chairs. While they looked narrow, when I sat, I noticed that they were plenty wide enough for my ample hips. Another thing that I didn't often experience.

"Is this okay?" Bob asked before giving us our menus.

I nodded.

"It's perfect," Sharon said brightly.

The menus came in fancy black folders that had Derry's in gold script across the front.

Inside was a hand written page of specials and another typed list of items that seemed to go on forever.

"Order whatever you like," Sharon said. "Don't worry about the prices. And if you don't see something on the menu, order it anyway. They're very good about being able to accommodate anyone's special needs or tastes."

I nodded.

I was hungry and the pasta they had on special with a mushroom sauce and sausage, chicken, and artichokes sounded perfect. I didn't look at the prices because Sharon told me not to, but I figured it was far less than the steaks a waitress brought out to the people a few tables over. And honestly, as a fat woman, I worried far too much about what people thought of me around food all the time, so it was hard not to overthink all my food choices and the prices thereof.

An old woman, looking older than Sharon, her back hunched over and her hair pure white came over to fill our water glasses. She looked too frail to be working.

"I'm Edie," she said smiling. "I help out from time to time at Derry's. I haven't met you before."

She didn't hold out a hand, but her eyes twinkled as she looked at me.

"I'm Holly Baxter," I said.

"Nice to meet you. Sharon is probably giving you the spiel and you look about as believing as I did when I came here a couple of years ago. You'll get used to the island," Edie told me. She set the pitcher of water on the table for a second, paused, then lifted it again and walked to the back of the restaurant.

"Edie is interested in everyone," Sharon said. "She could easily be retired here. She gets a decent enough check from social security and we, on the island, wouldn't allow her to starve, but she loves bringing around water and chatting everyone up. She lives in a little house near the police station."

"Are there places to rent here?" I asked.

Sharon shook her head.

My face must have fallen.

"A house chooses you," she said then.

I raised my eyebrows, about to ask more, but a middle-aged woman approached. Her hair was dark brown, highlighted with purple and cut short above her ears. The black pants and white button-down shirt were quite form fitting on her, accentuating her breasts and hips.

"Hi, Sharon," she said.

"Hello, Mindy," Sharon said. Her voice dropped a bit on Mindy's name as if she didn't quite approve of her.

"I'm here to take your orders," Mindy continued. She waited for Sharon first.

Sharon ordered a fish dish that I hadn't noticed, but then again, I'd been checking out the specials figuring those were the cheaper meals. I ordered my pasta. Sharon ordered a diet soda. I got an iced tea to go with mine.

Mindy left and Sharon watched her go.

"I'm just not sure how much longer she'll last here," Sharon said. "She's gotten herself in a lot of magical trouble. Trying things she hasn't been trained at and heaven forbid she should ask someone. I know Damien is fit to be tied by her."

Considering I thought Damien was creepy enough to have me considering not taking the job in the first place, his dislike of Mindy was a mark in her favor. For the life of me, I couldn't see what a nice woman like Sharon would see in a man like him.

"Anyway, you were asking about housing," Sharon said bringing the topic back. She didn't quite get to finish when a man walked over to our table.

He was tall and thin and had the darkest skin I'd ever seen. His hair was clipped so short his skull peeked out. He wore blue jeans and a dark pullover. He didn't have a gun belt, but something about the way he walked suggested he was used to one.

"We've found a body," he said stopping at our table.

"Recent?" Sharon asked.

Her lack of concern surprised me. I would have been much more distressed about someone finding a body than Sharon appeared. Maybe she didn't react to many things.

The man shook his head slowly. "Marie thinks it's close to a hundred years old, but she'll have to do some date testing on it."

"Thank you, Xavier," Sharon said.

My arms started to tingle. I rubbed at them. When the tingling stopped, Xavier was gone and my food was in front of me. Sharon's drink had been refilled and I couldn't remember any of it.

A sudden fear slipped through my mind. Maybe it wasn't so much talk about magic as something that was happening to me. Perhaps I was losing my mind.

Chapter Four

My food smelled deliciously of garlic and sausage. I heard
the clink of silverware on plates and the soft music that
had been playing in the background all this time. Around
me, the restaurant had added diners. Four people, all
women, sat in the booth right next to Sharon and me. I
hadn't noticed them come in.

My stomach knotted as I worried what was happening
to me. Before my mother died, she'd had some petit mal
seizures. She'd lose time. I wondered if that had happened
to me. Not only did it frighten me from the point of view
of health, but I worried what Sharon had thought if I had
sat across from her slack-jawed and unmoving.

"You're fine," Sharon said. "It didn't seem appropriate
to have you involved in a crime discussion on your first
evening here so I put you to sleep."

I frowned. I didn't feel as if I'd woken up.

"It's a spell," Sharon continued. "I think you'll feel
better if you have something to eat or drink."

My ice tea waited for me, the ice partially melted.

I picked up the glass, thankful that my hand wasn't

shaking, that I felt strong enough to pick up the glass at all, and brought it to my lips. The cool tea brought me back to myself.

"You're just fine. It was my mistake in putting a spell on you that you wouldn't recognize. I try not to do that, but sometimes I forget. Aging," Sharon said with a sigh. She shook her head.

"Now about your house…"

She paused to take a bite of her food. The smells coming from mine were enticing now that I wasn't worried I'd just had a seizure. Although, perhaps I had and Sharon was using the idea of magic to cover my illness. I wondered if it was possible the people here knew I had these tiny seizures even if I, myself, did not. Were they playing me? Perhaps hoping for money? If so, they would be sadly disappointed.

I listened as Sharon talked about houses choosing a mage. I would walk through empty houses and one of them would decide it liked me. Any house could form itself to what I wanted. If I wasn't interested in yard work, there were people who lived on the island who were paid to do that.

"Just like in the outside world," Sharon added.

I nodded.

"Tomorrow," Sharon said, "Bernice will come and get you started on spells. She'll get a measure of what types of magic you have the most affinity for. Then she'll introduce you to Jack at the accounting office and he'll show you around there. The rest of the week will be getting familiar with the office and learning some magic. If, at that time you decide to stay, we'll formalize everything."

"So, it's like a week-long interview?" I asked.

Sharon laughed. "I suppose it is."

I wasn't sure what to say. Job interviews were stressful

enough. The idea of a week-long interview felt horren-dously overwhelming.

"Except, of course, you're interviewing us. You're welcome here simply because it's our place to teach you how to use the magic you're coming into," Sharon said.

I swallowed and thought about the small carry-on I had brought. A couple changes of underwear and an extra shirt plus a nicer outfit for interviewing. Not much to wear for a week. I hoped that my things dried quickly as I'd be doing some hand washing.

"It didn't look like you brought much. We need a better way to welcome people to the island, but it's so difficult to know. Some people have enough magic to see the job posting but don't have interest in learning more or just aren't ready. They can't find where to go so it seems wrong to offer the job right then and say bring a week's worth of clothing. Besides, would you really have wanted to know you'd be interviewing us for a week?"

"Maybe say a weeklong trial?" I suggested, although I wasn't sure I'd have gone for that, either. It would have felt weird. At least I'd have had more clothing if I did go for it.

"Bernice will take you shopping for clothes in the morning. She always does. People tend to bring more formal clothing to interviews and we're really not formal here," Sharon said.

I looked down, certain there wouldn't be clothing for me in that shop. I usually wore a 28 and even stores that carried plus sized clothing usually stopped at 22 or, on rare occasions, at 26. I could sometimes wear a 26 but I wouldn't count on it.

"Don't worry about sizing. That's one of the wonderful things about Jewel. Carl can fit you in anything you like," Sharon said.

I frowned not sure what she meant but I wasn't going

to start out a potential job by whining about how I couldn't fit into standard-sized clothing. I'd make do with what I had and if I could grab another top, so much the better.

Sharon didn't try and persuade me to believe her and changed the subject, telling me more about the island. I wasn't supposed to ask mages where they got their powers. I shouldn't volunteer what I thought my own reasons might be for having powers as it would be possible to use that against me.

I listened and asked questions now and then. Outside, the night was getting cloudy and the stars were no longer so bright. It wasn't long after I finished my pasta that Sharon decided we should leave.

"Don't we have to pay?" I asked.

She waved a hand at the waitress. "She'll put it on my account. I'll get the bill later in the month. In fact, you'll probably see it before I do if you take the job."

I nodded. If the restaurant was going to allow people to charge meals, it seemed like it would be easier for them to do the billing, but I wasn't going to start out by complaining. There was a lot to the island that I didn't understand, starting with the whole magic thing.

We walked up the hill towards the B&B. Sharon sighed. "As I get older, I've come to hate this hill, but the island hasn't ever changed it. I'm not quite certain why."

I didn't quite know what to say to that, so I added nothing.

At the B&B, Sharon paused by the garden. She made no move to go in. I noticed that the three cats were on the porch, cuddled up.

The white one raised its head to look at us.

"The cats can go where they like," Sharon said. "If they want to go inside, let them. Of course, if you don't like cats, you don't need to let them in your room, but the B&B belongs to those three and the calico."

I thought it was an odd turn of phrase that the B&B belonged to the cats, but I didn't really know how to question her. Instead, Sharon waved me off and headed the final length up the hill to what I assumed was a plateau of some sort. Three houses that looked like homes, but could be businesses sat between the B&B and the top of the hill. Across the way, was an open space, like a park, overlooking the lake. It would be a wonderful place to have lunch if it wasn't private property.

Inside, the B&B smelled of garlic and onions and I wondered what they'd served, or were serving, for dinner. Not that I was hungry, but the smells were interesting. I noticed a very old man sitting alone at the table across from the door. He hunched over an empty plate, the blue and white plaid napkin still rolled on the plate. Water sat near the plate in a large glass not unlike the glasses at Derry's.

The tables that sat cuddled in the bay window were all filled. One with an Asian woman and a white man about my age and another with two older women. The conversations were low murmurs. Ian sashayed out to the old man's table with a pad and pencil and asked him what he wanted.

I looked away, noticing the calico cat watching me, not from under the writing desk, but from on top of it. She held my gaze as I walked towards her. I reached out a hand to let her sniff.

She turned away from me and leaped back down, slipping into her hiding place. The other cats had been equally uninterested in me. Not fearful, but not that interested. I sighed and went back to my room.

While it smelled of burnt candles, nothing was out of

place since I'd left. I had a lot to think about as far as taking the job. Of course, I had a week to give them my final response about whether or not I'd stay. Maybe everyone needed that time to decide if they could live with the strange beliefs that pervaded the island.

The bathroom called to me, the large rounded soaking tub perfect for a long stretch of debate. I quickly undressed, carefully folding my clothing seeing I'd probably have to wear the same outfit over and over. The tub was full of water at the perfect temperature when I finished that task. I groaned in pleasure when I sank down into the water. After a quick wash, I let my mind wander.

By the time I got out, my skin had wrinkled into prune territory, but I was far more relaxed even if I didn't have answers. Climbing into the soft bed, I was asleep before I was aware of pulling the blanket up over myself.

I awakened only when I heard a scream outside my room. I sat up, waiting, but silence greeted me. Looking at my cell phone, I noted it was a bit after six, early morning light just barely creeping in around the edges of the blinds. My heart still thudded, wondering who had screamed, but with no other noises, I had nothing to follow. Instead, I started dressing before going to find out what was happening.

Chapter Five

The calico cat greeted me at the door when I walked out. She purred at me and wrapped herself around my legs. I bent down and petted her. She raised her head, bumping it into my hand, her mouth opening slightly in pleasure. I'd rarely had a cat so happy with me.

"Aren't you a sweet one," I said softly.

I'd decided to wear my nicer blouse but with the same black jeans I'd arrived on the island in. Those would allow me to wear more comfortable shoes. It sounded like there might be walking involved in between learning magic and working at the office.

I had no idea if I could actually learn magic or if Sharon was a little bit off. I hadn't quite bought into the idea, although the experience at the restaurant had gone a long way to getting me to accept the unusual, especially the stairs.

In the bath, I'd realized that I'd looked down at the rooftops of the buildings on the lake side of the street from higher than just the second story of a building, much higher. I hadn't felt any movement from the bottom of the stairs to the top. Just one moment in one place and the next in another. No machinery could do that, at least not that I knew of.

Still, it could have been a trick.

I pushed myself up from petting the cat, knowing that someone had screamed and if someone were in trouble, I wasn't doing anything to help. I wanted to help, even if I didn't know what to do.

I walked out to the dining area. Two men in flannel shirts sat at a table laughing. They didn't seem to have noticed the scream, or if they did, the problem had been solved. The one on the side closest to the kitchen had a short, clipped, red beard. The other had dark hair and was clean shaven. Both, however, were large men, easily able to have portrayed Paul Bunyan in a local play.

"You're up early!" Ian said, appearing from the kitchen. While he seemed to just be in front of me all of a sudden, I knew he'd walked over. I'd just been busy noticing the two men.

"I thought I heard a scream," I said.

"Just Darla," Ian said.

I raised an eyebrow wondering if Darla was prone to screams that I'd be hearing the whole time.

"Her talent seems to run to seeing ghosts and she saw one that scared her this morning. I guess it wasn't one she knew," Ian told me. Then he gave me an impish smile.

Someone who could see ghosts was afraid of them. It hadn't occurred to me that there would be talents that I might not want. Not that I really wanted magic. I mean, in daydreams, magic sounded good. Imagine being able to create however much money I might need, or force an employer to hire me, or even have a body that was more culturally preferred than the one I had.

The idea of having magic, if it were real, felt like an

inordinate amount of responsibility I wasn't sure I was ready for. There were so many ways magic could go wrong, so many factors to think about. I worried that in creating my perfect job and spelling an employer to hire me, I'd take away the last chance for someone else. I'd watched enough *Twilight Zone* and stories like that to worry that having the body I'd always dreamed of would come with an unexpected and very much unwanted cost.

"Would you like to sit by the window?" Ian asked. The shades were mostly drawn but I could see pink light coming through.

"That would be great," I said. "I don't suppose we can pull up the shades?"

Ian shook his head. "Darla said the ghost is outside so she won't come out of the kitchen if the shades are open and she's the one who's supposed to be serving."

For the first time, Ian sort of dropped the complete happiness at doing everything and looked a bit frustrated. He shook it off and turned over a clear glass tumbler for water. A pitcher sat on a table just a few steps away and he poured some.

"This morning, our chef has prepared eggs with four cheeses and scallions and we're serving them with crisp bacon, an English muffin, and a Swedish pancake. Does that sound okay?" Ian asked.

The last part was said almost in a whisper as if he were afraid that I'd say something horrible about it.

"It sounds wonderful," I said.

"And you can have coffee, tea, or hot chocolate, as well as your choice of fruit juice," he added.

I ordered coffee and orange juice which was probably boring, but Ian took that down and sashayed back to the kitchen. His walk was really something and I wondered if he came by that naturally or if he practiced.

I looked down under the mostly lowered blind. A bird bath sat next to the window with low bushes of lavender around it. Something else crowded in, but I couldn't tell what it was. No birds hovered in the bath, but it was early morning in the fall. Chances were the birds had all headed off south to find warmer weather.

A few minutes later a youngish girl with red hair in a long braid came out. She had an apron over her clothing. Her look was as closed off as Ian's was open. This had to be Darla. She didn't seem happy to be working at the B&B and I wondered how much of that was a dislike for the work and how much was because she'd seen a ghost.

I mean, I can't imagine that I'd look perfectly fine if I saw a ghost. I'd be terrified.

Darla didn't say a word as she set my coffee down on the table. She didn't plop it down, at least. She left without even a greeting. The two big men who sat at their own table chuckled as she went by. Darla turned and glared at them, shutting them up.

While I didn't appreciate her attitude, it didn't seem right for others to be laughing at her. I sipped my coffee before adding in some sugar. I liked a bit of milk or cream in my coffee as well, but no one had brought that out so I set the coffee aside and waited.

The steam was just beginning to dissipate enough to make my coffee appear to be a drinkable temperature when Darla brought out two plates of food for me. She set them down and was about to head back into the kitchen when I asked for milk or cream.

"Which?" Darla demanded. She didn't sound too pleased at having to be out there longer.

"Whichever is easier," I said.

"Pick one," she demanded.

Ian hurried out of the kitchen. For once he didn't walk with the trademark sashay. He didn't look pleased.

"Darla," he said, his voice holding an edge.

Darla said nothing. She just fled to the back.

"Really, which do you prefer—milk or cream. We have both and they're equally easy," Ian said. "I should have asked when you ordered coffee, but I'm not usually around quite this early."

"Cream is always a treat," I said.

"Then you should have a treat," Ian told me. "Don't let Darla get to you. She's not much of a people person on her best days. If I had to guess, I'd bet that some of her power comes from accepting that she hates the rest of humanity."

Making a face, Ian left. I hoped he'd bring the orange juice when he returned. I nibbled at the very crisp bacon he had promised. It was perfect.

He was back in no time with the orange juice and a little silver pot of cream.

"Thank you so much," I said.

"You are very welcome," Ian assured me. "You have no idea how much everyone is looking forward to having more people at the accounting office again. Jack is nice and all but he's easily overwhelmed. And we've all sent our billing and payroll off to the office—we don't do it in-house like a lot of places—and it can get frustrating waiting."

"I hope that I can help," I said. I tried not to glance down at the eggs and bacon, but they smelled so good that I couldn't help it.

Ian took that as his cue to leave.

When I finished, I headed out onto the front porch. I'd made some progress with the little calico. Now I wanted to meet the other cats.

The morning was nippy but my shirt was warm

enough for a short moment on the front porch. A woman sat on the bench next to the plants where the cats had been lounging, but for the moment, none of them were around.

The woman turned to face me and I stared into the empty eye sockets of a skull.

Chapter Six

I gasped, my lungs too tight for an actual scream. The skull
was part of a skeleton, rotting clothing clinging to the
bones. It had looked like someone wearing an outfit
because I'd not expected to see a skeleton.

"Holly." The voice came from everywhere and
nowhere. As the skeleton had no vocal cords, it might have
been my imagination.

I stepped back, pressing myself against the door. I felt
around for the knob, wanting to run, but my hand shook
and I couldn't seem to find it. This had to be a nightmare
or another trick.

"Be careful," the voice said. "Your potential is strong
and he will see it."

And then the skeleton in the ragged clothing was gone,
leaving a fading impression of a woman in the sort of old-
fashioned house dress that my great-grandmother might
have worn.

I breathed in as deeply as I could and then out again,
trying to calm the racing of my heart.

The white cat peered out from under the bush in the

garden and ran up to me, twining its body around my legs. I squatted to pet the cat. The softness of its fur grounded me more than I would have expected. I wondered if the cats had magical powers, too. After all, cats had always been associated with witches in legends, so perhaps in this strange place, cats could do things as well as the humans.

I stood when the white cat was tired of the attention and headed back down to the tree where it joined its friends.

I turned to find the knob on the door and turn it. I had planned to sit out on the bench but I couldn't make myself go over there, where the skeleton or ghost or whatever had sat.

If this was what Darla saw when she saw ghosts, no wonder she screamed and had no interest in going outside. In fact, no wonder she wasn't pleasant to be around. I'd be grumpy, too.

I moved slowly into the front sitting room. Part of me wanted to go back to the privacy of my room, and, though the walk wasn't far, I wasn't sure my legs would hold me. They were trembling, not the muscles exactly, but something deeper, as if the skeletal creature had taken something vital from me and I needed to rest after confronting it.

The sitting room held several wide flat chairs. I could have sworn that when I came in the other day those had been wingback chairs. But they were all lavender, cream, and green which were the colors I recalled. Perhaps in my imagination a Victorian ought to have wingback chairs and not these modern things that looked less inviting, but were certainly wide enough for the likes of me.

I sank into one, letting my eyes close as I continued to breathe deeply. However long I sat there, it was long enough for someone to arrive at the B&B and let themselves in.

"You must be Holly," a voice said.

I opened my eyes and looked toward the entry. A tall, rather thin woman stood there. Her skin was dark, though not nearly as dark as Xavier's, and her white hair was shorn short and combed upwards.

"I am," I said.

"Tired already?" she asked. The woman, who had to be Bernice, had a habit of acting as if she were looking down her nose at me.

"I was up early and then I had something of a scare," I said.

"What sort of scare?" She moved into the sitting room quickly. Her movements were light and easy. Though up close I could see the age spots and fine lines across her face, from a distance I'd have mistaken her for a twenty-something. Even her clothing, the skinny jeans and heavy turtleneck sweater suggested a younger person than she appeared to be.

"I went outside to sit on the bench. Watch the lake. And someone was there, I thought. But when it turned, it was a skull and it was wearing only rags. It knew my name," I said.

"It spoke?" She seemed shocked.

I nodded.

"Ghosts don't normally speak," she said. "Are you certain it wasn't your imagination?"

"I don't have a clue," I said. I mean this whole island could be my imagination. From my point of view a ghost speaking wasn't any weirder than anything else.

She watched me, frowning. I wasn't sure if she was frowning because she didn't like my answers or what.

Finally, she walked further into the sitting room and settled on one of the wide chairs and leaned forward.

"I'm Bernice and I'm supposed to teach you to use your magic. If you're going to be working with spirit, I'm probably not the best teacher, but Sharon told me that you were very good with fire."

"I almost burned down the room trying to light a candle," I said glancing over at her. It wasn't that I believed, completely, that I had created that fire, but I was interested to see how she reacted to the idea that I might have been able to burn down the room.

"Sharon had to get up and move her chair when she tested me," Bernice said smiling suddenly. "It was that fast."

I filed away her comment about "testing" and nodded.

"I can do earth quite well and water. I am average at air. The one element I have no real connection to is spirit," Bernice said. "It's unusual for a mage to have a strong affinity for more than one element, but many of us have weak affinities for several."

I nodded. I wondered if I ought to be taking notes. I almost asked, but Bernice looked away.

"The most unusual is when someone has a strong affinity for spirit. Usually, those who see spirits work on the spirit level and do little with other elements. Sharon will be very interested to hear about your talent," Bernice said.

I bit my tongue to stop from asking about Damien. I wanted to know what Bernice thought of him, if he was as creepy as my initial impression of him.

"Let's go outside band see what we can do about earth," Bernice said. She left the room without waiting for my response. I had no choice but to follow. She seated herself on the bench the skeletal creature had been sitting on. The idea of it being a creature felt better than calling it a skeleton which evoked a sort of playful Halloween influence. This creature had been anything but playful.

I waited, leaning against the rail, but only after checking to be sure it was solid.

"You are welcome to sit next to me. I don't bite." The smile Bernice gave me suggested she wanted to make an innuendo about biting, but had barely refrained from doing so.

"That's where the ghost was sitting," I said softly. I glanced around. I didn't see the cats.

Bernice nodded. "I'd get used to sitting where they were if you can see them. They turn up in all sorts of places if Darla is any indication. Damian has a moderate affinity for them as well, though, like you, he's one of the unusual mages that can use other elements. I believe he said that over the years it's become easier."

I wondered how long he'd been a mage but was sort of afraid to ask. I didn't want to know Damien or even know about him. It didn't surprise me that he could see spirits, though. He looked so much as if he were a walking dead or undead person himself.

Bernice sniffed. "But let's focus on earth."

She put me through paces of creating a flower, first from my imagination and then asked me to copy something she created. It wasn't easy and by the time we were done, I felt as if I'd gone on a ten mile hike.

"Now let's focus on water," she said quietly.

She went inside to grab a bowl for me, though I was a little surprised she hadn't just made me create one.

I started to nod off and then felt someone beside me. I looked over expecting Bernice, but it was the ghost again, still skeletal but a bit of flesh covered its face.

"Better?" the voice asked.

I shook my head. The empty eye sockets that appeared

black in the daylight and the strings of flesh and hair were worse than the plain bone.

"It is difficult to rebuild what I once was for your eyes," the creature said.

The idea of rebuilding itself didn't sound like something a ghost would have to do.

"Ghosts as old as I am have to be rebuilt. My body was the first, though any traces of the killer are gone. Let them know there's another body in the field, another one murdered like the others. The police have always known that it happens and while they look, the bodies are always old by the time they're found. The magic holds all of us, but holds me the most deeply," the creature said.

I frowned.

"You have to find it. It's the only way."

The creature faded into a shadow of itself, changing into an older woman even as it faded and was gone as quickly as it appeared. Bernice walked through the door with a dish.

She sat in the exact place the creature had been.

"It's cooler out here," she commented. "The seasons change so quickly. I expect we're in for a long winter."

"The ghost was here again," I said. "She said I need to go to the police and tell them they have to find its body. It said it's the only way."

I watched Bernice's face. She didn't give anything away, not a widening of the eyes or a tightening around her mouth. She said nothing.

"First, let's see what you can do with water. Then we'll go to the police," she finally said, holding the dish.

I got to work on creating water. It took longer than creating a flower, even copying her example, and when I finally managed it, I barely filled the bottom of the little dish. If I had to rely on myself to create water when I was thirsty, I would die.

Bernice shook her head. "I guess in a pinch you can do it. Let's return the dish and get started."

I stood up and immediately felt dizzy. I held onto the rail and stumbled towards the door. Except there were two doors now and I could hardly focus on either of them. Everything appeared as if it were in a great fog.

Bernice entered through one of the doors and I aimed for it, managing to grab onto the handle in time to keep from falling forward. My weight pushed it inward and I stumbled inside.

Although I barely tripped, I didn't have the coordination to stay upright. I landed on my hands and knees. If I had eaten anything with Bernice, I'd have wondered if she'd poisoned me, but I'd been outside on a bench the whole time.

I heard footsteps walking quickly towards me.

"How many spells did you have her do?" Ian asked.

I tried to look at him, but my neck was stiff and I could hardly move.

"We did the flower exercise and then I made her copy mine. Then she tried for water. It wasn't much," Bernice said. She sounded put out.

I felt long fingers helping me sit upright. I smelled something spicy. A faint trace of aftershave, perhaps. Ian was there.

"You're holding something back," Ian snapped.

"She sees ghosts, but they come to her, so that shouldn't have drained her," Bernice said. "Not that it's any of your business."

"The guests at the B&B are always my business," Ian snarled. He got me as comfortable as he could, sitting up, leaning against the wall.

"Darla! Bring us out a clove and cinnamon tea with milk and sugar."

I closed my eyes. The tea sounded wonderful.

A few moments later my arms started to tingle and I rubbed at them.

Then I smelled the scents of the tea, spices that made my mouth water. I really wanted to sleep but that scent was amazing.

"Just open your mouth a little," Ian said quietly. "I'm going to give you a sip of this."

I did as he asked. The tea was every bit as flavorful as the smell had led me to believe. I sighed when it was gone.

"Another sip," Ian ordered. I took another one, which perked me up enough to open my eyes.

I still felt as if I'd walked all day and all night without stopping. My body wasn't just fatigued, it literally ached with exhaustion, making it hard to get comfortable. The floor felt too hard and the wall dug into my back.

I shifted a little.

"It's probably uncomfortable as we get some energy flowing back through your body, but hold still," Ian said. "Bernice tends to skip the part about knowing when you've overdone it. Magic takes energy out of the user. As you use it more, your stamina will increase so you can do more spells at once, but in the beginning even a couple of spells can be too much."

He offered me another sip of tea.

It perked me up even more. The ache softened, though it didn't go away.

"Can you hold the cup?" he asked, studying me.

"I think so?" I said.

He helped me at first. I took another sip. It tasted good and it made me feel better, as if I could move.

Bernice leaned against the far wall, pointedly not looking at us, almost as if I were faking this.

Certain I could hold the cup on my own, Ian backed off a bit. "You'll want to finish that before you try and stand. I'll get some toast going. That will help ground you."

"Thank you," I said.

"It's nothing," Ian told me. "It's not like I haven't had to do this before." He shot a look at Bernice who sighed and looked up at the ceiling as if she were being put upon by even being there.

I wisely said nothing and sipped the tea which had to have something more than the spices, sugar, and milk the way it was perking me up. I just didn't know what that might be.

Chapter Seven

When I finished the drink, I tried standing up. Ian stayed around to help. Bernice stood aside, her eyes still looking up to the ceiling as if I were making a big production out of something that should be nothing.

I felt my face heat, not just because of the exertion of standing up, but also from embarrassment that I was clearly not up to what was expected of me. I knew this was an old wound for me, being a fat woman. I had been fat even as a child and to prove myself I had always pushed in physical education, making sure I wasn't as slow as my body needed to be. I hated it when I couldn't keep up and there were times when I couldn't.

We had a round of gymnastics once and I had failed that miserably, although I had done okay on the balance beam. My body wasn't made for some of those moves. I hadn't been laughed at, which was almost worse because deep down I feared it was because the other kids hadn't really expected anything else from me.

"Let's go into the dining room," Ian said, his hand steadying me as I walked. I felt his hip bump against mine as he walked and he gave me a look and then winked like he'd done it on purpose.

He settled me at the first table and then went and got some toast and orange juice. "Remember spells will always take energy out of you, especially at first, so eat lots to keep your strength up."

"Thank you," I said, gulping down the juice. It helped but not like the tea. "What was in the tea?"

Ian shrugged and smiled. "Nothing special. We add a bit of ginseng which is good, but I know a spell or two that helps as well."

"I wondered about healing," I said, taking a small bite of toast. I realized that my stomach wasn't exactly settled, not after nearly fainting. I didn't want to overdo it and end up vomiting.

"We have an actual doctor here," Ian said. "You'll like her when you meet her. Everyone does."

I wasn't sure how objective Ian was. He seemed to like everyone. Although he rolled his eyes at Bernice and wasn't afraid to call her out, he still seemed very fond of her.

"While there are certain things that require a bit of magic, we rely on the doc more than anything. If there's an emergency, magic can stabilize someone. My magic tends to lend itself towards supporting and healing the body. Judy, the acupuncturist who used to work on the island, always told me I should study medicine, but it's not that interesting to me. I like to talk too much." Ian shrugged and smiled again.

I gave him a small smile as I took another bite of toast.

Bernice wandered in and sat across from me. "If the ghost thinks you need to tell people about it, then we need to hurry and get to Xavier."

"You talked to a ghost?" Ian asked.

I nodded.

"Was that before or after you were working with Bernice?" he demanded putting a hand on a hip.

"Once before and then once when she went in to get a dish for water spells," I said.

Ian raised his head and looked over at Bernice, frowning.

"She's fine," Bernice snapped.

"She talked to a ghost," Ian repeated. "No one talks to ghosts. That's like beyond Darla and her thing is Spirit. She can't stop seeing ghosts and Holly talked to one and you continued on with her lesson as if it was no big deal?"

Bernice shrugged. "She's fine. She's had tea. She's eating."

Ian glared. "I'll go get you some more tea. No special magic this time, but it will warm you up. I know Darla gets cold when she works her spirit magic."

With that he left the table, though something in the swing of his hips told me he wasn't pleased with Bernice.

Bernice didn't look at me.

"You teach everyone?" I asked, hoping that was a safe topic.

"I'm good at imparting information," Bernice said and then offered nothing else.

"You don't like me," I said. I didn't know where that came from. Lots of people didn't like me and mostly I didn't care. I wasn't sure I liked Bernice, either.

"It's my job to push you," Bernice said. "It has nothing to do with like or dislike. I don't know you."

Ian returned with tea. "And knowing Bernice, she won't care to. None of us know her except in her role as teacher and the fact that she paints some amazing pictures. But she doesn't share."

I sipped at the tea. I was going to live in the bathroom

later on, what with my usual coffee, two cups of tea, and two glasses of orange juice.

Bernice glared at him. "I'm a private person."

"And you make it hard for students to really learn anything because you make it clear you don't like questions," Ian said. "A teacher ought to welcome questions."

"I teach the way I was taught," Bernice said quietly. She didn't seem particularly ruffled by Ian's comments. I had a feeling she'd heard them all before—perhaps even each time she brought a new student and started teaching.

"And maybe that was wrong and you ought to adapt," Ian said.

Bernice said nothing. She stared at him. I worked on my tea. Even without Ian's magic, if he really had magic, I felt the warmth of the liquid and the spices filling spaces inside me I hadn't known were empty.

When I set the cup down for the last time, Bernice stood.

I followed, though I paused to make sure I was steady on my feet. While I felt more tired than I thought I should be, I wasn't in danger of falling over or passing out on the way to the police station. Sharon had said something about it being around the corner at the bottom of the hill. I thought I could make it.

I followed Bernice out into the garden. The day was still crisp with clouds coming in from the west. We'd probably have rain later, unless the island had a way of fending off rain. I thought of asking Bernice, but she walked quickly down the hill ahead of me. I can usually pick up the walking pace pretty well without much effort, but I had to work to keep up with her, particularly given the tiredness in my limbs.

Ian was right. Magic could take it out of you. Either that or the elaborate tricks and schemes they had on the island had tired me out. It seemed like it would be more work to make someone believe in magic if it wasn't real. Deep down I knew I believed. My attachment to finding other explanations had more to do with protecting my ego from being taken in, so to speak, than it did with any real belief that this wasn't happening.

I wrapped my arms around my chest as I hurried down the hill. I noticed lights on at Jewel Accounting. I figured I'd be going there later on. An Asian woman came out of one of the buildings near Derry's—the outside gave no inkling of what it was—looked over at Bernice and hurried up the hill. The road continued over the plateau and I wondered what was beyond it.

Maybe if I wasn't so tired, later on I could go for a walk and explore. People had to live somewhere and most of the buildings on this road seemed to be businesses even if they looked like houses.

Even the grocery store could have been a long low ranch house at one time, albeit a ranch that had been extended and widened from its original form. A group of three people went inside while others came out. I recognized one of the flannel-shirted men from the B&B that morning. A woman with dark curly hair wearing a flowing skirt followed him, though it was clear she wasn't with him. She smiled at me, but ignored Bernice.

I wondered if Bernice had taught her and she had hard feelings. Or maybe Bernice had made it clear that she didn't want people talking to her. I had no idea.

We rounded the corner. The police station was made of brick and wood and was literally *just* around the corner. I noticed spotlights placed on the corners of the building that focused on the gravel lot that surrounded the place. A road, narrower than the one that went uphill, went past and then curved away from the hillside as it rose, into the interior of the island.

I didn't see a single car in the lot, though I did see a couple of scooters, one in bright pink. Bernice hurriedly cut across the gravel to the building. Closer up, I noticed windows with reflective glass sending the sun glaring back at me.

Bernice opened the door and walked inside.

I expected a body scanner at the door, but the island had nothing like that. Instead, the door opened onto a waiting area that looked more like the waiting area of my DMV than anything I expected in a police station. Several blue plastic chairs sat along the wall that held the door. The floors were white tile squares worn down to cream.

A few steps away was a large wooden counter. A very old woman stood behind it, her face so wrinkled that I could hardly spot her eyes and nose. She stood bent over the counter, her face turned up to see us.

"Holly saw a ghost and I think Xavier needs to hear about it," Bernice said.

The old woman peered around Bernice at me and her head bobbled. It kept moving up and down even as she shuffled around the corner to talk to someone.

She shuffled back, her back still bent, her head still bobbling around as if once it started she was powerless to stop it. She gestured around the corner.

Bernice headed that way. She reached behind the low wood gate that kept out unwanted visitors and opened the latch, then twisted to the side to hold it open for me. An unusually polite thing for her to do.

I'm not tall, but even I had to bend down slightly to hold the little gate open. It certainly wouldn't keep anyone out. A tall man could have leaped it. Given the right incentives, I suspected even the old woman could have leaped it.

Bernice led me around the corner to a large room with several desks. In the corner nearest the door a single desk was off in a cubical. Xavier sat behind it.

I noticed the same golden-brown wood on the desk as made up the front counter and even the floors at the B&B. Perhaps the island grew only a certain type of tree that stained that color. Or, more likely, someone had gotten a certain color of stain delivered to the island at one time and this was everyone's choice.

Two other men and a heavyset Black woman, her skin a few shades lighter even than Bernice's, sat at other desks. She looked up at me and smiled before turning back to a computer.

Xavier stood up and gestured to two chairs I hadn't noticed before. They were slightly around to the side. Bernice plopped down in one and I took the other. They were the same plastic chairs as the ones out front, only these were brown instead of blue.

I sat gingerly making sure the plastic wouldn't break off when I sat, but it held me. In fact, the chair was wider than it looked, curving around my hips in a way that wasn't uncomfortable at all.

"You saw a ghost?" Xavier said.

I nodded.

"It spoke," Bernice added. She gave me a look as if I were supposed to know how important that was. Of course, both she and Ian had made a big deal of it so perhaps I should have, but this was all new to me. I'd never even reported a crime before.

"It spoke." Xavier repeated the words as if he thought he'd misheard. No question lingered in his inflection.

I nodded.

"What did it say?"

"That she hasn't been found yet. That you need to find

her skeleton to stop what's happening," I said. "She said something about being the beginning." I had a hard time remembering the exact words. Those had seemed important at the time but I hadn't had a chance to write them down and then nearly passing out flushed the conversation from my mind. In fact, if I hadn't told people I had talked to a ghost, I might have doubted it had happened, thinking it was only a dream.

"What did she look like?" Xavier asked.

"She was a skeleton," I said. "At one point, as she faded out, I thought I saw an old-fashioned dark plaid housedress."

Xavier made a note. "But no features that you could share?"

"I only glimpsed her face. She seemed grandmotherly?" Like that was going to help them. It's not like the skeleton would have a sign on it that said "grandmotherly skeleton."

Still Xavier wrote down what I said.

"Did it say anything about where it was buried?"

I shook my head. "Only that she hadn't been found and it was important that that happen."

Xavier sighed. "If you see her again, please ask where we should start looking. The bodies we've found have been all over the island in fields. I can't just go around digging up the entire island."

"Aren't there devices that do imaging and stuff. Like metal detectors, but for bodies?" I asked.

"We make sure our residents are comfortable," Xavier said. "The money goes there. Specialized detectors for skeletal remains is not on the list of items we've purchased. There's no real need. I suppose if you have significant spirit magic, perhaps you and Darla could locate where the skeleton is or point me in the right direction."

My eyes widened. I hadn't even considered that this might come back to me having to do more work. Not that I was afraid of work, but my sense from the ghost was that this was important and I didn't have a clue what I was doing.

Chapter Eight

Bernice stood abruptly from her chair after Xavier made that suggestion.

"My student is not ready to try contacting ghosts," she said. She didn't even look at me, just started to leave.

I stood more slowly, giving Xavier an apologetic look before turning to follow. The old woman watched, though her head had finally stopped moving. She was close enough that I smelled the faint scent of roses.

Bernice was already across the room. She pushed open the door and I felt the chill breeze with it. Rain was well on its way.

"Hurry up. We need to get to Derry's before it starts to rain," she said.

I hurried behind her and out into the day.

"Can't you teach me to reach ghosts?" I asked. "Or at least help me get strong enough to contact her?"

"No." Bernice continued walking quickly across the gravel. In no time we were on the road and hurrying up the hillside.

I waited for her to say more, but no such luck. The

people milling around outside the grocery store were gone, though I did see a few people inside, heads above the signs and boxes that lined the windows.

A gust of wind whipped around me, pulling my hair and trying to keep me from walking up the hill. Bernice leaned into it and kept on going, just as quickly as before.

I tried to keep up or at least not fall further behind. The wind died down after that single gust and walking was easier. The impending storm made the air feel damp and I was sorry I'd left my sweater at the B&B. I hadn't thought we'd rush out and I wouldn't be able to grab it.

Bernice seemed unaffected by the weather, but she had on a heavier sweater than I did. Nothing seemed to phase her. A few large splats of rain hit the pavement before we made it to Derry's. I practically ran inside to avoid getting wet. Moments after the door shut, I heard the rain start to fall harder. Bernice had already disappeared up the stairs.

I followed. I was surprised to find the little alcove now dressed in white wood with bright red ribbons decorating a chair rail. Inside the restaurant everything was brighter than it had been the previous evening.

Bernice stood near the podium waiting. This time an androgenous person waited at the podium. Their face was lightly wrinkled with age, their hair white though I couldn't tell if that was dyed or natural.

"This way." Even their voice was in a midrange that made it impossible to assess their gender.

Bernice followed them to a table across from the booths. Instead of the dark vinyl on the booth benches and seats of the chairs, the color was bright red against white tables. The tables themselves looked like old-style white Formica tables with silver edging. The chairs, too, had silver on the edges. The floor was covered in white laminate, though I could have sworn it had had wall to wall carpet last night.

Two red place mats sat across from each other with red-checked napkins. The little rounded chairs that looked too small for me surprised me when I sat. They held my butt just fine. Bernice, at her height, didn't seem to have a problem getting her knees beneath the table either.

"This looks really different from last night," I said. "How did they change it so quickly?"

"Magic," Bernice said. "If you only have one restaurant in town, don't you think we'd get sick of it?"

The idea of completely changing the interior of the restaurant had never occurred to me.

"Is the menu the same?" I asked, glancing down. This wasn't the elegant hand printed menu from the night before. This was a long, laminated sheet covered with items on both sides. Everything about the place had a retro diner feel.

"Of course not," Bernice said, frowning at me as if that was the dumbest question I had ever asked.

"The chef must be really good," I said.

"Magic, again," Bernice said. "While they don't just magic the food into being, they can magically make sure they know how to make whatever it is the customer wants and make it correctly. Magic brings us real food, but that can take more work so most people try and order off the menus because those things use items that are sure to be in stock."

I nodded. It all made sense, if I believed in magic.

A middle-aged man, his gray hair combed back over his head though his face was unlined and his eyes danced in youthful pleasure took our orders. I'd barely had a chance to look at the menu but the soup, salad, and sandwich looked good. I got French Onion Soup and a turkey and Swiss cheese on rye.

"Make sure it's a whole sandwich and not a half," Bernice said. "She's new at magic and had some trouble this morning. Ian would kill me if I didn't make sure she ate enough."

The waiter smiled and nodded. "I'm Gerald, by the way. I'll probably see you around."

"Holly," I told him smiling back.

Once he was gone, Bernice leaned forward. "I wouldn't turn my charms on him. Not only is he only a waiter, he and Carl at the police station are a couple which means even if they break up, you're not his type."

"I didn't think I was turning my charms on him, as you put it," I said. I sipped from the water glass that had been filled before we even sat down.

"It certainly looked like it, the way you were smiling at him." Bernice made a face and a sound like a humph.

She acted like a jealous woman and it made me wonder what kind of relationship she had with Gerald. He'd been nice enough to her, but nice in the way a waiter is nice to any customer. However, that was better than most people treated Bernice. I had a feeling, given the way she acted, that was on her and not the other people on the island.

We sat in silence for a few minutes. With other people the silence might have been comfortable. I felt my skin crawl a bit with Bernice, questions itching to come out, but I wasn't certain if she'd answer them or if she'd snap at me.

Finally, I could stand it no longer.

"Do I work at the accounting office later today?" I asked.

"I'll take you over there. Jack will show you around and

give you an idea about what you'll be doing, but you won't be working. I'll take you down to the clothing store, too, so you can get some more clothes for the week."

"I doubt they'll have my size," I said. One thing about Bernice, I had no problems just blurting out what I wanted to say.

"They have everyone's size. David just waves his hand over whatever you pick and it's your size. He has good earth magic and this is a way he can be of service on the island. Before that, he worked as a minister so being of service was a big deal to him." Bernice made it sound like being of service was a bad thing.

"The island doesn't have churches?" I asked.

Bernice waved a hand. "Once, I guess. But it's not so popular now. Most people just leave the island to go. And there are so many little sects and divisions, we'd have to have a dozen churches where only one or two people would go. David does have a worship service every other Sunday in the B&B but it's pretty plain so that anyone of any faith, Christian or otherwise can come. We had a couple of Jewish families that did a Torah study group one evening, but they've left the island."

"What about other faiths? I'd think that pagans would be here."

"You mean witches?" Bernice said.

I nodded.

Gerald came back with my salad. Bernice had gotten a burger but she had a side salad as well. Both were larger than I expected. I'd have to make sure not to eat too much otherwise I'd gain even more weight. I doubted David would want to keep expanding my clothing, although it was nice to think that someone could if it came to that.

"We have some," Bernice said. "But witches are witches and we're mages. Being a witch doesn't guarantee our sort of magic, though they do their own spells. Being a mage doesn't require that you suddenly start worshipping nature or anything either."

I ate a bit of salad thinking about what Bernice had said. The lettuce was crisp, the tomatoes more flavorful than I expected at that time of the year.

"Does magic make the food more flavorful?" I asked.

Bernice narrowed her eyes a little and smiled a conspiratorial smile. "I think it does but Sharon swears that it doesn't work that way."

I nodded, smiling back, sharing our secret. Maybe Bernice really did just need a friend.

Just then Bernice's expression faded. She looked down at her salad and started to breathe deeply and slowly as if trying to calm herself.

I started to turn.

"Don't," she hissed.

The room got quiet. I felt eyes watching something I couldn't see. My back was to the door. The rain meant that the reflection in the window wasn't terribly bright. Someone had come in.

After what felt like an agonizingly long time where I heard only the occasional clank of silverware being set down, people began speaking again, though the murmur seemed lower and less natural than before.

"What?" I whispered.

Bernice shook her head.

Gerald seemed more constrained as he brought my soup and sandwich and Bernice's burger.

Bernice began shoving food into her mouth as if she hadn't eaten for a week. I ate as quickly as I could but I'm so used to trying to not eat fast to minimize what I ate that it was hard to persuade my mouth to chew at high speed and for my throat to swallow.

Just as I thought I was catching up, Bernice put down one of the French fries on her plate. The room went quiet again.

A tall, thin man dressed in black appeared at my side. He smelled of too much aftershave, something that tickled my nose and made me want to sneeze, though I held it in.

"Bernice," he said. Without looking up, I knew it was Damien.

Chapter Nine

I would have never have believed Bernice could look or act nervous. If anything, she always appeared too calm. But not now. Now her hands fluttered around the dishes, pink crept into her cheeks and she bit her lip before answering.

"Damien," she said. "This is Holly Baxter."

I looked up and prepared to nod at him.

Damien, however, was still staring at Bernice. I watched as she gulped. I actually heard the sound. Gerald stood over near the bar, leaning back against it as if trying to avoid getting too close to something I couldn't see.

"I know. I took part in her interview," Damien said. "I've heard that you may have overworked her this morning."

Bernice looked away, not responding.

"You know Darla tells me things," he said.

Bernice nodded. She didn't gulp this time.

My mouth felt dry just thinking about what it must take to frighten Bernice. And she wasn't just frightened. She was terrified.

Damien took his time looking down at me. "But you seem none the worse for wear."

"No," I said, biting off the need to add the word 'sir.' I wasn't a child and he wasn't my father or my boss, no matter that Sharon had said he was sort of the power behind the mayor.

"A ghost spoke to you?" Damien said.

The room went even more silent than it had been, if that were possible. If the walls could listen, they were listening now.

"It did," I said. "I think."

"You think?" Damien repeated the words slowly, quietly.

"I think so," I repeated. "I've heard that ghosts don't speak, so it's possible I was so overwhelmed seeing one that I thought…"

Damien closed his eyes and drew in a breath. The silence stretched into torturous lengths.

"I think you did talk to a ghost, but these others have made you doubt yourself. That's not good." Damien's glare turned on Bernice. She seemed to shrivel before my eyes.

My hands were sweating and, as I tried to force a breath into my too-tight chest, I felt my heart beating as quickly as if I'd just run across the island trying to save my life. Maybe my heart was trying to do just that by running away from Damien.

"What did the ghost say?" he asked.

"That its body hadn't been found," I repeated. I didn't know why I called the ghost an it for Damien but a she for everyone else. "It said that was important. I told Xavier about it."

"Xavier." Damien said the name as if he didn't know who I was talking about.

I wasn't sure how to reply. Didn't want to reply. I

wanted out of there. My stomach threatened to bring up all my food.

"I'm sure he'll keep me informed if your ghost helps him find any other bodies. It doesn't quite seem worthwhile unless it becomes a nuisance to you, though there are ways of banishing ghosts," Damien said finally.

He left the table without saying good-bye.

Considering the clamor that picked up after a few seconds, I could only believe that he'd left the building. I didn't speak until I saw Bernice straighten up in her chair and breathe out a sigh that sounded like nothing so much as relief.

I turned to look around, making sure he was gone. As I'd suspected, he was nowhere to be seen.

"I didn't think you'd be afraid of anyone," I said as softly as I could. My mouth was dry. I sipped some of my soda.

"Only those things that could hurt me," Bernice said. "You'd do well to mind that."

I wanted to ask more, but she gave the faintest shake of her head. No doubt there were people here who might overhear whatever she might say about him. I held my tongue.

We finished our food quickly. I had things I wanted to ask Bernice, but didn't dare, not in that place. I barely tasted the food though I thought that when we started it had been good, no better than just good. Excellent.

Bernice led the way out of the restaurant. Like Sharon, she didn't stop to pay and just walked out. I hurried behind her, surprised that she waited near the door downstairs.

"This is as private as it gets," she said, keeping her voice low.

I felt a tingle down my arms like she'd done magic.

I rubbed them and gave her a questioning look. The

only sound was the rain hitting the glass. While a new urn filled with umbrellas had appeared in the corner, I doubted they'd be much help.

"I just did a spell to keep our conversation private," Bernice said but she kept her voice low.

I nodded at her, hoping she'd tell me something important.

"Don't ever get on the wrong side of Damien. It's best not to be noticed. He's been here as long as I can remember and I think Sharon said he was here when she arrived. He acts as if he's the reason the island has magic, but I know enough history of magic to understand that's not true, as does anyone who's spent any amount of time in other enclaves," Bernice said. She started to say more, but stopped.

I found that interesting. "He sat in on my interview," I said.

"He sits in on all interviews. He doesn't do anything, really. Sharon might be mayor but there's no question Damien is in charge," Bernice said, her face scrunched in dislike. It was the most emotion I'd seen her express.

"He's not a vampire or something, is he?" I asked.

That made Bernice laugh. "I realize you're new and magic probably seems like something out of a fantasy world, but no, vampires aren't real. Not like you mean. Besides, as nasty as it is outside, it's still daylight and we aren't even lucky enough to have to worry about him only at night."

I smiled. At least we had something in common.

My arms tingled again. Bernice frowned.

"Is someone else doing magic?" I asked.

"I am," Damien said, appearing from nowhere behind Bernice.

Chapter Ten

I said nothing. I hoped that Bernice's spell had kept him from hearing us. I didn't like that he'd been standing there, hiding from anyone who came down, perhaps trying to overhear things.

"And what were you doing, skulking around?" Bernice asked. Her words were brave but there was the faintest hint of a tremble in her voice.

"I was waiting for the rain to pause," Damien said. "And then suddenly you came down and needed to have a private conversation. I so hate it when people try and keep secrets. What magical secrets were you imparting to your student?"

Bernice kept her head up, but she had no response.

"She was teaching me how to keep things private in a public place," I said. "I had questions about our food, but I couldn't ask them upstairs."

"Was it not to your liking?" Damien asked.

I shook my head. "Just interested in the magic, but Bernice didn't feel good about talking about it there. In case someone took offense or something."

Bernice said nothing. She didn't move.

"This wasn't more discussion about the ghost that speaks to you?" Damien pressed.

I shook my head. That, at least, was true.

Damien kept an eye on me, assessing me for a reaction. "No one in all the time I've been here, and believe me, I've been here longer than anyone, has ever spoken to a ghost."

For my part, I had no idea what sort of reaction I ought to have. I mean, I remembered talking to a ghost. It had spoken to me. I had no idea why.

"Bernice doesn't teach spirit magic. She has none," Damien said. "I should take over your lessons."

"Holly has exceptional fire magic," Bernice said. "So I think we'll be fine. You know mages need the basics before they even start on spirit magic."

"We'll see," Damien said quietly. He grabbed one of the umbrellas and stepped out into the rain, giving lie to his reason for being back there.

Bernice clenched her jaw. I noticed she flexed her hands as well. She waited until he was out of sight before grabbing an umbrella.

"Take one," she said. "I know it looks like it won't be much help at the angle the rain is falling, but they're spelled."

I did so and followed her out.

Surprisingly enough, the rain didn't hit me. It came towards me but appeared to hit something at the edge of the umbrella and slid down as if the shield were glass.

Bernice didn't wait for me to watch and be fascinated by the event. Instead, she turned and headed up the hill towards the accounting office, forcing me to hurry after her.

The rain drummed against the umbrella. I wasn't sure if it was actually hitting the material or just the sides of whatever magic was protecting me from it. Whatever it was, it made a sound that echoed around me.

My feet got wet walking up the street from the tiny streams that had formed when the storm started. The road had looked smooth when the sun was out, but now I could see every crack and imperfection, a topological map of lakes and rivers.

Fortunately, the office wasn't far and Bernice waited for me on a covered porch. She'd closed her umbrella. Once I got there, she opened the door and went inside. Her umbrella dripped but she quickly added it to an urn by the door. Like the one in the restaurant this one was white stone and stood almost to my hip and, if it were empty, would be wide enough for me to climb inside.

I stowed my umbrella and looked up, stunned at the view. Windows formed the entire back wall of what might have once been a living room. Nearest the door sat a desk and chair. Beyond that a single carpeted step led down into what once might have been a huge conversation area. A rounded fireplace sat on the inner corner, all golden wood and white brick. Sofas with blue and green cushions were built into the conversation area and two long benches sat in front of the windows.

The view from the entire space was amazing. I'd come there just to look out over the lake.

"It's something isn't it?" a very short man said. He'd appeared from a hallway on the left that I hadn't even begun to notice.

I nodded.

Bernice walked into the room and settled on the sofa. "You can show Holly around," she said, waving him away. Apparently, she was as captivated as I by the view, not that she was willing to admit it.

"I'm Jack," the short man said, holding out his hand.

I shook it, realizing we were just about of a height. I'm not particularly tall, just wide. Jack was short and very slender. Dark hair, with enough gray to give him the ability to claim "distinguished" as a description, framed his face.

His clothing fit well, though his button-down shirt was wrinkled and not particularly fashionable. He could have walked out of a photoshoot of accountants from 1950 if only he added a tie.

"Holly," I said.

"I'm a bookkeeper," Jack said. "I haven't kept up my tax license, so with Rachel gone everyone had to send stuff off-island, which was a pain. We do some things that aren't standard."

I nodded.

"I'll show you around," Jack said. He turned back down the hall he'd appeared from. The beige carpet continued and the padding beneath let my feet sink into it. If I lived in a house like this, I could lay down in the conversation pit and roll around on it for hours.

The room that might have been a bedroom in the front of the house was a store room. Shelves lined the walls. A built-in island of drawers sat in the center creating a table that held a three-hole punch and an old fax machine.

Jack showed me where he kept boxes of paperclips, plenty of paper, extra pens, and the assortment of flotsam that offices require. If I could think of it, it appeared to be there, neatly stored and labeled.

He left the room and led me to a room the size of a bathroom that was filled with file cabinets.

"Old files and taxes," Jack said, nodding at me.

A lot of places just scanned documents and then sent them back to their owners but clearly Jewel Island was different.

He crossed the hall and led me to a tidy office with

another floor to ceiling window taking up the back wall. I almost missed the antique looking maple wood desk and the shelving unit with file drawers at the bottom, though they were all lovely and tidy enough to get a gasp of awe on their own.

"How do you get work done with that view?" I asked.

"You get used to it," Jack said simply. "This will be your office. Mine is next door."

Jack's was marginally smaller but the view was equally glorious. His desk held a set of inboxes, one of which had a single piece of paper waiting.

"It's a mess," he apologized, though I couldn't see a single thing out of place, unless he counted the paper a "mess."

Generally, I am not an untidy person, but if this as Jack's idea of messy, we might not be the best officemates. I'm much more laid back about things and sometimes, particularly when I'm busy, my desk gets filled with sticky notes and forgotten pens.

Leaving Jack's office, we walked back through the main room and into a small hall on the right. There Jack showed me a half-bath for us and for guests. The final room was a small break room. The breakroom had a door out onto a small deck that hung off the edge of the cliff upon which the building sat.

"I'm not sure how comfortable I'd be out there," I said, laughing.

"It's very secure," Jack said. "All up to code and magic adds to the security. The island doesn't let its people get hurt."

"But I heard about the body that was found in the field," I said.

We stood in the small breakroom, looking out over the lake.

"The dead body wouldn't have been a mage, not one that the island recognized. Bad things don't happen to us here," Jack said. His conviction made me want to believe him although I had to wonder if his belief was based on fact or just on the sort of wishful thinking that people often engaged in.

"I had no idea," I said.

"It's the way the island is. It takes care of us as we grow and accept ourselves and our flaws," Jack said.

I nodded and hoped that I'd get out of there before he started spouting some basic self-help stuff, or worse, started talking about how important diet was and then suggest I'd feel better if I were thinner. His tiny size suggested he'd never had to worry about what he ate.

Jack shrugged when I didn't say anything and he led me back out to Bernice. The whole "tour" had taken less than an hour and wasn't at all what I expected.

"I guess I'll see you tomorrow," Jack said, not looking at Bernice.

"I guess."

Bernice said nothing. The urn near the door was gone. When we stepped outside, I noticed that while the clouds still hung heavy and low, no rain fell.

"I guess it's time to get you some clothing," Bernice said and led me back down the hill.

At this rate I was going to be in the best shape of my life. I was thankful for my tennis shoes that let me do all that walking, even if my feet did feel a little damp.

We were almost to the bottom of the hill, where the little house with a sign that said *clothing* stood, when someone called out to Bernice.

Bernice turned and paused. I looked back to see Sharon hurrying down the hill. She was practically running. Her white sneakers were worn and the laces were poorly tied. I worried she'd fall and injure herself but she didn't have any trouble.

She paused to catch her breath for a moment when she reached us.

"Damien said he needs to work with Holly," she said.

"And I said that the elemental magic is the basis. He can work with her next week," Bernice snapped.

"He feels that with her talent for talking to ghosts that she'll need his guidance right away," Sharon said.

"You mean he wants to know what she learned in case a ghost decides to dish on him, right?" Bernice's voice held an edge. She wasn't making a joke at all.

Sharon sighed. "I wish you didn't hate him so much. Life would be so much easier."

"Damien isn't trustworthy and I don't have a clue why you can't see it. He walks into a room and everyone goes silent," Bernice said. "People are terrified of him."

"Not everyone," Sharon said. "People like Darla who have spirit magic and work with him come to trust and admire him."

"Or they're spelled."

I thought about what Jack said about the island not letting people come to harm. It didn't make sense that people would be afraid of Damien if the island would protect them.

Sharon shook her head, waving off Bernice's comment. "Let it go, Bernice."

While I wouldn't have said that I liked Bernice, she was far preferable as a teacher than Damien.

"Do I get a say?" I asked.

Sharon paused to look at me as if she'd never even considered such a thing. "Well, no," she finally said. "You don't know anything about magic, so how could you make a decision?"

"Bernice and I are settling into a working groove," I said. "It seems like changing teachers after one day isn't exactly good policy."

I had no idea what was good teaching policy, but I was certainly going to advocate for learning from someone other than Damien.

"I'm sorry Holly, but I think Damien is right. Anyone with your power over spirit magic needs a teacher who can guide you through that magic. While normally, I'd side with Bernice on having a good foundation with elemental magic, I don't know anyone who's talked to ghosts. You need to work with Damien. He'll come by in the morning instead of Bernice and you'll work with him."

Sharon then turned and trudged back up the hill, not waiting for further argument. Her hunched shoulders suggested she was less than pleased.

"I'm sorry," Bernice said.

I glanced over at her and gave a small smile. If anyone had asked me this morning if I'd be sad that Bernice was no longer going to be my teacher, I'd have laughed. But there I was, wishing she could continue and feeling sick at the thought that she wouldn't be.

Chapter Eleven

There wasn't much to do but continue on to the clothing shop. The building was smaller than I expected. Like the accounting office, it looked like it might have once been a house. A large front window looked over the street and I saw a man walking around arranging things. That must be David.

Bernice opened the door which came complete with a bell that rang when the door opened. A polite tinkle, not the horrible computerized sound that some had.

"Afternoon Bernice," the man I assumed was David said. He stood well over six feet and although Bernice was tall and thin, he towered over her. He wore nice khakis that fit his body well. He wore his very blonde hair very short around his ears.

"David," Bernice said. She didn't smile, but there was something in her voice that suggested David was one of the few people she was actually glad to see. Or maybe it was just relief that she didn't have to worry about Damien any longer.

I glanced around the store, noting the rack of clothing

along the back and the drawers along the side walls. A single cubical that might have been a dressing room waited. A counter with a cash register sat to the right and a platform with a couple of mirrors sat off to the left. A few comfortable looking chairs with tables sat in the middle of the room.

Soft classical music played in the background. Although there wasn't much of a view in the building, it was pleasant enough.

"This is Holly," Bernice said, turning to me.

David gave me a pleasant smile. "Nice to meet you," he said. "I expect you weren't planning on being here for long and now you need a few outfits."

"I do," I said. "Although, I understand if you don't carry my size."

David shook his head. "Doesn't matter. I get whatever size I can from wholesalers in the minimum amount of items. Using magic I can make sure they fit anyone. I can even change the colors slightly. I offer people the ability to special order whatever they want and I'll make sure it works for them. Usually if the color isn't quite right, I can fix that, although I can't change patterns. I can fix rips and tears if you need that as well."

"You do all that with magic?" I asked.

"Mostly," David said. "I can mend a few things, but I'd never make it as a seamstress. I don't have the patience. But for some reason this works for me. Maybe it was all the times I wanted pants that hung to the ground and mine didn't quite reach!"

I laughed a little.

"Look around and see what grabs you. Don't worry about the size. I'll make it fit. I can either measure you or I can use a standard size chart which I'll show you," David said.

I wandered to the back, wondering how the clothing thing would work.

"Underwear is over by the counter in the drawers," Bernice said.

"Thanks," I told her. I would need to grab a couple of pairs. Not that I had a lot of money left, which worried me. I'd been ready to say I could settle in on the island after a week, but if I had to work with Damien, I didn't know if that was something I could do.

I glanced at a couple of blouses, startled to see a bluish gray Siamese cat sitting on one of the shelves.

"Well, hello," I whispered.

"That's Delilah," David said. "She's been around this place since I've been here."

"There seem to be a lot of cats around," I said.

"Most of the cats here are magic," Bernice said. "Mostly. The other ones, normal cats that are brought to the island are attracted to magic. I've heard they can see the energies and like to stalk them as if they were hunting."

I let Delilah smell my fingers and then rubbed her ears, which she took as her due. I didn't know whether she was an ordinary cat or a magical cat and I didn't ask. I realized that the idea of a magical cat didn't surprise me.

I found two tops that would work for me if they were resized—not something I quite believed could be done. I probably needed to see it to believe it. I then found a pair of black jeans that could look like work slacks.

I stood over the drawers and found one for underwear. I pulled out a couple of new pairs. I'd still be hand-washing in the sink but at least I wouldn't be doing it daily. I also found a bra that looked like it might be sturdy enough once it was enlarged. At least I hoped it would be.

I handed everything over to David and he touched each item in turn. My arms tingled so I knew that magic was happening. After he finished, he handed me the jeans and the shirts and told me to try them on.

The dressing room in the far corner was roomy and had a long bench on which to sit. I pulled on the jeans first, surprised that they fit well. Finding jeans in my size was hard. These were a good quality. Even if I didn't want to stay there, I was going to be coming back to that island to buy clothing, no matter what the cost. They were a little big in the waist but I didn't mind that.

I pulled on one of the tops and it was a little tight under the arms. I came out and mentioned that.

David nodded and made a note on a piece of paper. I raised an eyebrow.

"I keep information on all the island residents and the sizes they need. Your jeans are just a hair loose in the waist, so I can fix that. I'd also shorten them maybe an eighth of an inch, too," he said. He made another note.

I nodded and went back in to try the other shirt. I particularly liked this one. It was fairly stylish and would make the jeans work not just for the office but for an evening out if so needed. The bright blues and purples that swirled on the front and the soft draped neckline made it very dressy. At home, I had a necklace with a gold leopard with purple stones for eyes that would look stunning with the outfit.

Again, it was a little tight under the arms and considering how blousy the rest of the shirt was, I was surprised.

Once again David made a note. I returned to the dressing room and retrieved my own clothing.

I handed him everything once more. My arms tingled again.

"That should do it," he said. "Come back if you need anything else."

"Do I pay you now?" I asked. I wanted to know how much everything was.

"The island pays for clothing the first week," Bernice said. "No worry there."

I wished she would have told me sooner. I'd have stocked up on more underwear but I didn't want to look as if I were trying to take advantage.

David gestured to me to stay close while Bernice walked to the door. "I added two more pairs of underwear and another bra. Let me know if you need more support and I'll toughen the fabric."

I smiled and nodded. He gave me a conspiratorial wink as I left the shop. Most people on the island seemed really nice. Even Bernice was starting to grow on me. But once again my good mood was destroyed upon thinking that I had to work with Damien.

Chapter Twelve

I woke the next morning about a half an hour before I'd set my phone alarm. When I went out to the dining area for breakfast, I noticed David was sitting in one of the tables near the windows. He waved me over before Ian could seat me somewhere else.

"Welcoming our new mage?" Ian asked when he arrived at the table in time to seat me and pour some water.

"She probably needs all the welcome she can get," David said.

"I heard that you'll be working with Damien," Ian said, looking at me.

I drew a breath trying to think of how to be tactful.

Ian jumped in, laughing, "Don't worry. No one likes him but he hasn't hurt anyone that I know of and I'm the gossip king! Orange juice and coffee again this morning? We're having eggs benedict, and believe me, they are to die for!"

I assured him that was fine.

"Do you have breakfast here often?" I asked David. As

the words came out of my mouth, I realized they sounded like a bad pickup line and I felt my face heat slightly.

"Only on eggs benedict mornings," David said. "When Ian says they're the best, he's not kidding."

Four women came in and got a table towards the middle. I didn't recognize any of them but they were all my age and older. Ian was one of the few people who seemed a bit younger. I hadn't seen any children.

"Are there no children on the island?" I asked as Ian brought my coffee and refilled David's cup.

"No," David said.

Ian had already sashayed off to offer the other table coffee. He'd barely finished when a man and woman came in holding hands and took a table off to the side. The woman eyed me a little before leaning forward to talk to her breakfast partner.

"Why not?" I asked when the pause got long enough.

"No schools," David said. "And most children don't have shame to accept and those that do aren't usually self-aware enough to work on accepting it. That happens as we age. Ian started working on himself when he was quite young though he's older than he looks."

"So, people don't raise families here?"

"Again, no schools, so those that want children usually leave the island. It's easier that way. Of course, most people on the island and in the other enclaves are past childbearing age so there's that, too. Families want to be around other children and even if someone did have a child, there wouldn't be many here." David sighed.

I wondered if he missed having children around. I wanted to ask him about being a minister but Ian brought our eggs benedict out. The plate was larger than I expected. The poached eggs were perfectly done, the Hollandaise sauce an enticing shade of yellow. A small dish of oranges and apples sat to one side, fried potatoes and onions lay next to the eggs on the plate.

The food looked wonderful and smelled even better.

"If there's anything else?" Ian asked.

I shook my head. David shook his. I noticed he had a couple of rashers of that very crisp bacon on his plate that I didn't have.

"If you ask for anything, Ian will find a way to make it happen," David said in a whisper, as if he didn't want anyone else to hear.

The two men in flannel shirts entered and took a seat. They were quickly followed by a mixed group of four. Again, I didn't recognize anyone.

"What do people do on the island for fun?" I asked cutting into my eggs, watching the yolks run across the plate.

"We have a town center that has activities," David said. "It's just on the other side of the hill near the condominiums. We have plays, music, dancing. It's all small town stuff but it's there. Over by the police station we have a huge library. I haven't done any research but I expect it's as large as some of the metropolitan libraries that have multiple branches."

"Do the little enclaves of mages share books?" I asked.

David smiled and nodded. "We do. That started about fifteen years ago, I'm told."

I wanted to ask more questions but the food was good and my stomach demanding.

I was picking at my fruit, having finished the eggs when the door opened. While I wasn't sitting somewhere to feel the chill of the breeze, I shuddered as it did. The room went silent.

I knew without looking that Damien had arrived.

I heard the swish of cloth as he moved across the room,

the click of heels on the hardwood. No one said a word. David sat so still I didn't believe he was breathing.

"Holly," Damien said, reaching our table. He didn't even acknowledge David.

I looked up at him. My mouth was dry and I didn't have a clue what to say.

"I'd say you've had enough," Damien said, though there were still fried potatoes and fruit on my plate. My coffee cup was half full.

I wanted to protest but I waited for his next order.

"Come with me," he said. "Leave your coffee. Caffeine will interfere with spirit work and I need you focused."

I sighed, looking back longingly at my food and at David. While everyone else was looking down at their plates, much in the same way Bernice had looked at hers, hoping Damien wouldn't notice her, David looked up far enough to meet my eyes. Something in his gave me strength to follow Damien out of the room.

I hoped we'd leave the B&B so that others could finish their breakfast, but instead Damien led me to the sitting room. While I could hear the clink of silverware against the plates, no conversation flowed into the room. People were still avoiding his notice.

Damien gestured for me to sit in one of the chairs. I did so, my back straight and my feet firmly on the ground.

He nodded his approval at me. "At least you have good posture," he said.

I said nothing. The "at least" bothered me, as if he didn't approve of anything else about me.

"Where have you seen this ghost?" he asked.

"She showed up outside on the porch," I said.

"Let's see if we can bring her here," Damien suggested.

If I were a ghost and knew he was around, I wouldn't show up, but I didn't say anything. I worried both about failure and success, not certain which would be worse with him as a teacher.

I waited for him to do something. He stared at me for some time, his eyes boring into me. I didn't feel any magic being raised. We just sat there.

I tried not to meet his eyes but they were always there, staring at me.

"You do have an interesting way of focusing," Damien said. "Did Bernice teach you that?"

"Bernice only had one day. We worked on earth and water," I said. "I don't have a clue how to summon a ghost," I replied.

"If you were able to see her outside, you ought to be able to bring her here," Damien said. His voice held an edge. "I'm beginning to think you aren't trying."

"I don't know how to try," I said. "I just got here. I have had no experience with ghosts except that one appeared to me and maybe talked to me out on the porch. It was there earlier. Darla saw it before I was even up."

Damien's expression didn't change. Compared to him, Bernice emoted like a stage actor.

"Very well," he finally said. "Close your eyes."

I did so. I hated thinking he was looking at me while I had my eyes closed. At least I'd know if he were doing magic. And Ian was just in the dining room.

The door opened and a slight breeze blew into the sitting room. People were talking. I noted three voices. They stepped inside and went silent. I heard them leave the entry and the door closed behind them. If Ian made his money on the eggs benedict breakfast, he was going to be disappointed. I hoped he didn't hate me for bringing Damien to the B&B.

"Now, think of the ghost. I want you to picture her," Damien said.

I glommed onto the word her. Damien knew the ghost was a she. I'd said 'it' when I'd been around him. I wondered what he knew.

It was possible I'd slipped up but I'd felt uncomfortable giving him any extra information. For some reason it seemed important to keep him as far out of the loop as possible. Not that I could do much now, given that he seemed intent upon teaching me something.

I tried to picture the skeleton. In my mind, I built the ghost, the clothing threads, the black hollows for eyes.

"Leave me," a voice said in my mind. "Let go."

My eyes popped open. If I were used to ghosts and contacting them, maybe I could have played it cool and not let Damien know anything had happened, but a normal day for me had always been about adding and subtracting numbers and organizing spreadsheets.

"What happened?" Damien asked.

"I thought I heard someone," I said. I hoped it was vague enough.

"Did it sound like the ghost?" Damien leaned forward. His breath smelled sour with a hint of onions and garlic on it. Probably not a vampire, then. Not that I believed in vampires, not really.

"I don't know." That was a lie. I knew it was the ghost. Or my imagination. Maybe I didn't really know. I'd heard the voice in my head, that much was certain.

Damien's eyes narrowed fractionally. While his expression didn't change, he knew or at least suspected the lie.

"Try again," he demanded.

I closed my eyes. I thought about cartoon ghosts that I saw in images online, the old sheet covering something with holes for eyes going boo. I built up one of those and focused on making that real. Warmth flooded me and I relaxed into it.

"Stupid!" Damien snapped.

I opened my eyes. Before me stood a cartoon ghost in a sheet. I would have laughed if anyone but Damien had been sitting across from me. I'd created the ghost I'd been thinking about, unintentionally.

"Do you take me for a fool?" Damien demanded. He stood up, making him tower over me. His eyes blazed. I'd gotten a different expression out of him but it was not one that I wanted.

"I was trying to determine what a ghost looked like," I said. "My mind must have wandered."

Naturally I'd managed to make the first magic I'd ever done something that would get me in trouble. That seemed to be the story of my life. My face burned.

"And you thought it would look like this?" Damien waved his hand at the fake ghost I'd created. He knocked it over easily. Cardboard.

"You idiot girl! You probably lied to Bernice to get out of lessons. Admit it!" His voice had risen and then become a mere hiss.

"I didn't lie," I said. "There was a ghost out there. It was skeletal and frightening."

Not that he would care. Maybe later, though, if he complained I could use that as an excuse for not focusing on the ghost I needed to focus on.

Damien gave me a long look, again. His eyes didn't calm, though. In a movie, they'd still be red, like those of a demon. In fact, if I were brave, I'd take a photo with my phone and send it off to Hollywood and suggest that he play the monster in the next horror film.

"Close your eyes," he demanded. "And focus on the ghost that scared you. Focus on her so hard she has to appear."

I closed my eyes. I did not, however, focus on the ghost.

She didn't want to appear and I had no desire to force her. I let images of all sorts of ghosts run through my mind. Some scarier than others. I thought about the ghost, wondering if she could stay where she was and talk in my mind.

I can do that, she said.

Who are you? I asked.

My name was Ann Rodgers.

Was it Damien? I asked.

He takes. Ann said in my mind.

I'm supposed to focus on you but don't appear. I hoped that knowing she wasn't supposed to appear would help. I had no idea if it would or not.

He will take you. It would be a nice finish. Every few years, a new girl. I feel you, though. Not like the others, Anne said.

I thought I came here because I had magic.

We all came because of the magic, Anne replied. *But when he takes an interest, it means he'll use you, drain your magic, offer your body as a sacrifice on the full moon.*

Does Sharon know? Does anyone? I asked. I couldn't believe everyone on the island was complicit. I couldn't in a million years see Ian as being a part of this. And David. He was a minister.

He lies very well. And because he's been here longer than anyone, no one really challenges him. Even those who know he's been here too long for it to be natural. He needs to be destroyed.

How? I asked.

Find me. That's the answer. She'd said that before. I wasn't sure how finding her skeleton would help.

How will that help me?

I am the first. His magic still resides in my bones. It all goes to me and my bones. I am buried the deepest, buried the longest. He is linked to me, which is why I still haunt the island. Others have seen me but no one has been able to hear me until you.

Do I have to destroy your bones or something? I didn't understand what needed to be done.

I will help when you find them.

And then she was gone. I felt her leave my head. There was an emptiness where before there'd been a fullness.

I continued breathing, visualizing and discarding all sorts of ghosts. I did linger just a bit on this ghost though I tried not to focus too hard. I didn't inadvertently want to call her here to Damien. I had no idea what his powers entailed. Besides, if he thought I was useless maybe he'd leave me alone.

"You're not concentrating," Damien snapped.

I opened my eyes.

"I've been trying. I'm not used to this. I'm used to working with numbers." I doubted he'd care. Damien didn't seem as if he was much interested in caring about anyone else.

"Go to your room. Search your stupid computer or your phone or whatever and figure out how to meditate. I'll be back tomorrow."

Damien stood up and glided out of the room nearly silently. Only then did I heard the voices in the dining room start again, this time in whispers.

Chapter Thirteen

I stood up slowly, intending to head back to my room, but Ian came out of the dining room.

"Are you okay?" he hissed in a dramatic stage whisper.

"I survived." I tried to smile as I said it.

"Tea." Ian gestured to me to follow him. I noticed that David had slipped out at some point. In fact, only a few people were still in the dining room.

"I'm sorry that I brought Damien. He seems to have made the breakfast less than successful."

"They'll just be all the more pleased next week when we serve them again," Ian said, his usual charm coming back.

He left for a minute and came back with a cup of tea which he spelled while he stood by the table. "It's always best if it's done just before the person starts to drink it."

"Thanks," I said. I spoke quietly and while the women at the other table closest to me were talking, they also seemed very interested in what we were saying. "I'm not sure I did that much this morning."

"You created the fake ghost." Ian's eyes sparkled and he lifted his hands, shaking his head.

"Not exactly my finest moment." Damien wasn't likely to let me forget that ever.

"But it was awesome," Ian said. "Damien hates it when people don't jump to do what he wants. And I know you weren't trying to do that, but it was hysterical. I almost burst trying to hold it in until I got out back."

"I'm supposed to look up how to meditate," I said.

"If he'd let you work with Bernice for a week, you'd have known that," Ian said. "But that's Damien."

I noticed Ian glancing around. He opened his mouth to say something else, but Darla came out with food from the kitchen and he closed it without speaking. He turned and left. I had a feeling he had other things to tell me but wasn't willing to chance having Darla overhear.

I sipped my tea and looked out the window, wondering what I was supposed to do next. I glanced up at the clock, noticing I had two hours until lunch. I'd thought I wasn't supposed to go to the accounting office until noon but wasn't certain. Maybe Ian could help with that.

I waited for him to come back out but he never did reappear. Darla brought out all the rest of the food and bussed the tables as people left.

Finally, I got up and walked back to my room. The calico cat snoozed under the writing table. She gave a little meow. I squatted and petted her.

Her paw reached out and touched my arm. I felt the warmth from her toes and enjoyed the purr from her throat. I let my fingers find the sweet spot near her ear and rubbed until she seemed to tire of it. The whole time my arms tingled as if someone were doing magic, but I had no idea who that would be.

I stood up and went to my room, which I found had

already been tidied. I wondered how Ian did all that so quickly when it seemed to just be him at the B&B most of the time.

I pulled over my purse and started looking through my phone. I immediately searched the name Ann Rodgers, but of course it was such a common name that I got far too many hits. I thought my mother might even have had an aunt by that name, though I wasn't certain. Unfortunately, my mother had died a few years back so I couldn't even call her and ask her about it.

I texted my sister, Charlene, to see how she was doing. She responded quickly and asked how the interview went.

I let her know I'd be staying on the island for a trial run.

She sent me back a thumbs up.

Everything about the exchange sounded like my sister. If I needed to call someone, I could call her. She'd trust my judgement and let me come home if this got too dangerous. Of course, I wasn't quite sure how catching the ferry worked.

I paced around, wondering what to do next. Bernice might not have been the most talkative and easiest person to be around, but at least she acted human. And she'd explained what I needed to do even if she hadn't exactly been the kindest of teachers.

Finally, tired of the room, I left and went out to the sitting room. No one sat in the dining room, but Darla was wiping down tables and pushing in chairs. I wanted to ask where Ian was, but something held me back from doing so. Instead, I went out on the front porch.

The ghost didn't show up next to me on the bench. I wrapped my arms around my body. The breeze off the lake was colder than it had been the day before. I needed to go in and get a sweater. The cats that lived in the garden all looked up at me, ears up. The white one ran up the stairs and sniffed my feet. Whatever it smelled, it apparently didn't care for because it turned and left just as quickly.

The others stayed under the tree, watching me.

I got up and went in for a sweater. Darla was gone, but still no Ian.

I grabbed the heavy sweater and my cross-body bag and sat on the bench. I didn't have much of a view of the lake but it was pleasant enough sitting there, though I worried I ought to go to the office. Finally, I could stand it no longer and headed down the path towards Jewel Accounting. Jack could always send me away if I wasn't wanted there.

I passed an older woman hurrying along down the street. She glanced over at me and frowned. "Aren't you Holly?" she asked.

"I am," I said. "I'm sorry…"

She shook her head. "I'm Gretchen. I grow herbs and such. I thought you'd be working on your magic. Bernice didn't let you out early did she?"

At least I knew that not everyone got the island gossip the moment it happened.

"Damien wanted to work with me because I talked to a ghost," I said.

"Oh." Gretchen said. She said nothing else.

"He got frustrated with me and left," I added. "I thought I might check in with Jack to see if there was work I could start at the accounting office."

"But that's not how it's done," Gretchen said. "You need a mentor your first week. I mean, that's what Bernice does when she's not painting. I can't believe Sharon let Damien do that."

"She's the one who told me he'd be taking over.

Bernice even argued a bit."

A gust of wind hit us and Gretchen pushed back short gray hairs from around her face. It may have hung barely to her ears but it was thin and straight and the wind picked it up easily. My hair was likely a mess from the wind even clipped back in a barrette.

"I bet Bernice pushed back. She knows what the island expects of her. We all do. Damien isn't supposed to interfere with that, but this isn't the first time he's done so. I'm sorry. Let me take you over to the library. Sharon sometimes goes there and maybe we can get this straightened out. If Damien is frustrated with what you can and can't do, it's likely because you don't have the proper background yet."

Gretchen gestured for me to follow. Considering I wasn't exactly expected at work, I followed her. David had mentioned the library, and I had wanted to ask more but breakfast had come and then Damien had entered and we hadn't done much talking after that.

A few people waved at us as they went about their business in town. I even saw a woman coming out of Jewel Accounting. Gretchen waved. The woman was older, her hair permed and styled the way my mom had always worn it and she cocked her head as she saw me, frowning. Gretchen walked too quickly for the woman to ask who I was. I just smiled and nodded at her. She nodded back pleasantly.

Two men about my age came out of David's shop and hurried up the hill. Once again, they were friendly to Gretchen, saying hello but it was clear she was in a hurry.

She didn't cut through the parking lot of the police station. Instead, we stayed on the road until we got to a large rectangular building that looked like any small office building in a city. Made of mostly brick and wood, standing two stories tall, it had few windows except around the entry. Considering the size of the island, the building was larger than I expected.

Inside the little entry vestibule sat a bench off to one side and a row of pegs for those who wanted to leave their coats. Two heavy jackets hung on the pegs. Gretchen didn't stop to take off her own coat, pushing through another glass door to the main room.

The entry may have been tile but the main library was done in deep burgundy carpet. A large rounded desk sat in the middle of the room. Surrounding it, leaving only a path wide enough for a person to walk through were rows of shelving extending out like spokes on a wheel. A staircase with floating stairs ended on my right. Chairs were tucked behind desks or beside tables in sets of two or three in between the shelving and the stairs. The room smelled like old books and carpet cleansers. Soft music played in the background.

A woman sat at the desk, her hair perfectly styled, her makeup nicely done. She was more well-dressed than most people I saw around town and I admired the colorful scarf she wore at her neck.

Gretchen marched up to her, arms pumping. "I'm looking for Sharon," she hissed. Not exactly a whisper but at least she hadn't yelled from the front door. Not that it would have mattered. I didn't see anyone else in the building. Of course, if there were more chairs in corners, patrons could have been hidden among the stacks.

"I think she might be upstairs," the woman said, her voice rather deep and scratchy, like an old time sexy movie star. Her manicured fingernails, painted a perfect pink to match the print of the scarf she wore around her neck, tapped lightly on the desk.

"Great. Thanks Lauren," Gretchen said. She turned

towards the stairs.

I smiled at Lauren who gave me a slight nod before dropping her eyes.

The upstairs was as comfortable as below. The section that ran along the front, covering the entry held a long table for working and not much else.

Near the back of the building, I noticed another door. I frowned, wondering what it could be. It couldn't be an exterior exit on the second floor. Gretchen caught my look as she rounded a corner looking for Sharon.

"There's a hall to the second building out there. Each level has a meeting room. It's not as big as the activities room by the condos, but it's good sized," Gretchen said. "And, if lots of people want to meet, the meeting rooms have dividers so that you can have three meetings all at once!"

She bounced on her toes and brought her hands together softly in a silent clap. Everyone should get so excited about such simple pleasures.

After traipsing through most of the upstairs, we came across Sharon in a chair towards the back. She had a pile of books. Upon noticing someone coming, she turned the spines away from us, towards the wall and flipped the top book over. I wondered if she was a closet romance reader and was ashamed of her choices.

And here we were on an island because we'd come to accept certain parts of ourselves.

"Gretchen?" Sharon said. She didn't stand, but her expression held Gretchen at a distance. I'd like to think I'd have come closer, but I didn't want to brush by my companion who clearly knew how the island worked in a way I did not.

"Damien sent Holly off to meditate on her own without even giving her directions. She was walking over to the accounting office to start work when I was heading down to the grocery." Gretchen made it sound horrible that I was on my way to work. Most of the time that was a praiseworthy thing.

Sharon shook her head and then sighed. "Really, Holly. If Damien said to learn to meditate, you need to do that."

I wanted to ask how I was supposed to teach myself but Gretchen jumped in, clearly annoyed.

"You know very well Bernice teaches the techniques on her third or fourth day, after assessing what people can naturally do. Different students do best with different types of focus." Gretchen put a hand on her hip.

Sharon threw her hands up. "It's not like I can tell Damien anything, you know."

"You're supposed to be in charge," Gretchen said. "We've been without an accountant for almost a year. Jack was ready to quit over tax time because he was so stressed about everyone sending stuff out and the way Damien is treating Holly is atrocious and I wouldn't blame her if she left at the end of her week. We can't afford to lose her. We need an accountant."

"But Damien..." Sharon said weakly. She lifted a hand, her eyes pleading with Gretchen to understand.

Gretchen, for her part, shook her head. "Oh no. You took the job of mayor knowing it entailed working with Damien and you knew what that meant. Now you finally have to do something because Holly isn't getting the education she needs. That could go up to the U council and Damien won't like *that* either."

I had no idea what the U council was, but whatever it was Sharon's fluttering hands and the shaking of her head suggested that she wasn't pleased about them knowing. Maybe it was like a board for all the magical places or something.

Sharon sighed and stood up. She glanced at her books again but then headed towards the main door. Gretchen and I stood aside but Gretchen made no move to follow.

"Should I go with her?" I whispered. While Bernice had not made liking her easy, at least she made clear her expectations, however ridiculous they were. I had spent time working with difficult bosses. I could handle that.

Gretchen shook her head. "She'll go talk to Damien about making sure you get your usual training. Even if he has to split time with Bernice, that will happen. We can't have a half-trained mage around. I mean training is ongoing but there are some basics you need to have to avoid hurting yourself or others."

"When Sharon tested me, I did light the table on fire," I said.

"See?" Gretchen replied. "If you had been working on something on your own, you might have burned the place down. While the B&B would rebuild itself, people could have been hurt."

"Or the cats," I said.

Gretchen waved a hand. "They'd have gotten out, don't worry. The cats on the island are magic."

I wanted to ask what she meant, but Gretchen was turning to head downstairs. "I have to go to the grocery to deliver some herbs I've dried. If I were you, I'd head back to the B&B. There's not really time to work with anyone else this morning, but perhaps Bernice can come by and take you to lunch at Derry's and talk you through some basics on meditation."

At this point, that sounded good to me. Yesterday, I'd have dreaded another lunch with Bernice. Today, I almost looked forward to it. So long as Damien didn't suddenly appear to berate me for not intuitively knowing certain things.

Chapter Fourteen

Ian still wasn't around when I got back to the B&B. I sat in the sitting area and waited. I saw Darla come out a couple of times, but no Ian. I started to worry about him though I didn't know his schedule. Maybe he periodically took the time off after breakfast. It wasn't as if there had been many people around, so it seemed Darla would be able to handle it.

I kept telling myself that but part of me stayed worried and tense, as if some sixth sense was telling me he was in trouble.

I tried to remind myself that I was likely being dramatic, but my sixth sense wasn't listening. As a result, while sitting there, looking out the window, I couldn't settle. Had Bernice been there to talk me through any meditation exercises, I'm sure I would have failed.

No one came into the B&B during that time. The cats had disappeared from under the tree. I wondered about Bernice and Gretchen's comments that the cats were magic. I could understand them having magic, but being magic suggested they were made up of something other than flesh and blood.

The calico hadn't poked her head out from beyond the stairs when I came in. I considered getting up to look for her, but decided she was probably gone, too. I let myself wallow in self-pity, trying to decide if staying on the island was worth the trouble. All new jobs had downsides. Most didn't include a creepy vampire-like male with bizarre expectations.

Just as I was starting to think about heading over to Derry's on my own, Bernice came up the steps. She did not look happy, but I'd come to expect that from her.

I stood up to go to the door as she paused at the top of the stairs.

"I'm supposed to teach you to meditate while we eat lunch at Derry's," Bernice said. The tone of her voice suggested that was all my fault.

"I could skip lunch," I suggested. I was used to skipping meals, not only during tax season when it seemed like work piled up on my desk, but also from years of dieting. Easier to save calories for dinner or just not have them at all, not that that kind of eating had ever worked for me.

Bernice looked at me and shook her head. "I don't skip meals. Let's go."

I followed her out the door, thankful I hadn't bothered to remove my sweater. My purse hung lightly across my body.

We walked quickly down to Derry's, though I had a feeling Bernice did everything quickly and precisely. I was thrown a bit when we arrived upstairs and instead of the café from yesterday, I was greeted by a sort of casual pub-style interior. Worn wood walls and floors with square wood tables with angled red and white checked table cloths.

The bar stayed black like it had been in the evenings.

"I thought there was a café here yesterday," I said.

Bernice looked back at me. "I told you it can look however the manager wants it. You never quite know what you're going to get."

"Do they have a website or something so people know if they want to come in?" I asked.

"The island isn't that big so if someone takes offense to a certain style of dining they can always just go home and eat or grab something from the grocery store. In the evenings they can eat at the B&B." Bernice waited for us to be seated, which didn't take long.

The place felt crowded but the aisles were wide enough for me to navigate without disturbing anyone. A few people had burgers on narrow rectangular plates and others had large salads on oval platters large enough to have served turkeys.

We were seated near the far wall at a table with two armless chairs on one side and two chairs with arms on the other. Bernice took the chair with arms. While the chairs were wood with no padding, they were surprisingly comfortable. I could get used to this sort of magic. After we ordered Bernice didn't bother with small talk.

"Tell me what you know about meditation," Bernice said once we'd ordered and gotten our drinks.

"It's clearing your mind," I said. "I've done a bit of meditation where you count your breaths."

Bernice nodded. "When Sharon had you focus on your body testing your magical abilities to light candles, that's the sort of meditation that works best for simple magic. You'll want to focus on your body when you work with Damien."

"Are there other sorts of meditation?" I asked.

"Of course, and I get to those when I'm teaching but I

need to patch you into something you can use tomorrow morning. Damien will arrive just after breakfast, probably around 7:30 even though he says eight. I'll be there at eleven, which will give us an hour to work on spells for air."

"What if working with him wears me out?" I asked.

"Then we'll deal with it," Bernice said. "You need to think of working with Damien as an honor rather than a chore. No one knows spirit magic quite like he does. I've lived in other enclaves for a few months here and there, learning the way other places teach magic so I could be a better teacher and I've never met anyone who knows Spirit like he does. I've heard rumors about people in Europe, but my finances never allowed me to go there and learn."

"You'd think that Jewel would pay for that. After all, you are teaching people who come to the island," I said mildly.

"They paid for things in the States. I think it was decided that we had Damien as an expert on Spirit, so we didn't need anyone else," Bernice said.

I nodded.

"Have you seen the ghost since?"

I shook my head. I considered telling her what the ghost had told me, but decided I didn't quite trust her. Her sudden interest could just be playing good-cop to Damien's bad-cop.

"I did get a sense that the ghost was near but was sort of afraid of showing up with Damien around. Can someone with spirit magic banish them?" I asked.

"It's not impossible, but I think this one needs to find her body," Bernice said slowly.

I nodded. The ghost had talked about how important her bones were. Some link to Damien and whatever magic he'd performed.

"Is there any magic that we're not supposed to do?" I asked. "I mean working with spirits makes me wonder about things like raising the dead and all…"

Bernice shook her head. "I've never heard of anyone being able to do that. But if they did, it would definitely be one of those things that one shouldn't do. On the island, the island sort of dampens the ability to harm others, which isn't something that magic should be used for. Magic only knows those that have connected with it, so there are those who do questionable things, but even that is hard. Whoever murdered the people on the island had a lot of power."

I nodded. This was more than she'd told me yesterday. Details. I needed details. While I pondered that, Gerald, the server from yesterday brought out food.

"Why would someone with magical power want to harm someone? And it seems like it's been done regularly." I ate a bit of my shrimp tacos. Bernice had ordered them and they had sounded good. I was glad I'd changed my choice. Just enough spice and flavor without being overdone.

Bernice frowned at me. "I don't know. Perhaps the same reason people harm others in the non-magical world?"

"I think those reasons are emotional, like anger and jealousy," I said. "Or to get something like more money or to protect a reputation. That kind of thing. I know there are murderers who just get off on killing, too, but wouldn't having magic change the power dynamic?"

"Do I look like a killer?" Bernice asked. "This kind of psychology is not my area and certainly not something I can answer. I know that having magic allows me power that I didn't have in my former life. I don't have it in my life outside the enclaves. It's why I stay. There are few places a Black woman of my age is accorded quite the respect that I get here. I can be who I am and while many people don't like me, they respect me. I get paid what everyone else gets paid on the island—you'll find that out soon enough. All jobs pay a basic amount and then have small hourly stipends so that those working only part time get a little less than those who put in massive hours, as you're likely to around tax time."

I nodded. No wonder the pay seemed more than fair despite the fact that it was a small office. There was clearly some sort of supplement going on. I could probably rule out the need for money then, unless someone wanted to do something out in the world.

"The stipend only comes if you work on the island?" I clarified.

Bernice nodded. "Most people who live here work here, but there's one man who does IT for an off-island company and works from his house on the island. Another person is an artist and does crafts and sells them online. We had a writer for a few years. They don't get paid to live here, but the island is pretty affordable. All the enclaves are. It's not like there's that much demand to live here considering not everyone can find us."

"But internet gets here," I said.

Bernice shrugged. "If I tried to figure out the way everything worked on the island, I'd go crazy. I suggest you not go down those paths."

Which meant a lot of people didn't understand how the magic worked. Of course, lots of people couldn't really tell you how the power got from the power plant to their light bulb other than wires and such. I had no idea how wireless internet worked, but I knew people who did. Perhaps there were people on the island who did understand how the magic brought internet to the island. I could start by asking at the library, if I had time.

When we finished eating, the server took our plates and Bernice had me sit back and plant my feet on the floor.

"Count to five breathing in and then count to five breathing out," she said.

I did that for a few breaths, feeling a little silly sitting there in the crowded restaurant, conversations swirling around me.

"Focus on your breath and let yourself sink into your body," Bernice said just loudly enough for me to hear.

"When you're with Damien, you'll fall into a trance more quickly if you close your eyes, but this is a quick demonstration."

"I've done this sort of meditation when I was in yoga," I said.

Bernice gave a single nod. "Then you have the idea. Did you have any trouble concentrating on your breath?"

I shook my head.

"Then that's all you can do. If the ghost doesn't want to show up and have Damien see it, then it won't and there's not much you can do to force the issue. Damien has the power to force it all on his own, though he may not be certain which of the energies he can sense is the one contacting you."

"You said that most people with strong spirit magic don't have a lot of the elemental magic. It seems like I have fire and then this spirit magic," I said. "Is that odd?"

"It is a bit," Bernice said. She stood up. "However, just because something is uncommon here doesn't mean it doesn't happen. Even if it's uncommon in most enclaves, doesn't mean it doesn't ever happen."

She walked out of the restaurant looking around behind her. We went down the stairs, in that single step that just transported us down, and then went out the door. A man hurried by, nodding at both of us.

Bernice looked up and down the street. I felt a bit of magic on my arms.

"I can't sense anyone spying on us," she said. "It's possible you can connect with this ghost because there's a familial relationship between you."

I filed that away. My mother had had an aunt named Ann Rodgers. It meant nothing given how common the name was, but it left open the possibility that we were related. I opened my mouth to tell Bernice that, but then stopped and just nodded.

Bernice gave me a look as if she knew I had wanted to share but stopped.

"I think it's late enough for you to head over to the accounting office and get started," Bernice said quietly. "I'll be by the B&B midmorning."

I watched as she walked up the hill every bit as quickly as she'd walked down, her long legs moving quickly and easily, her back ramrod straight, head held high.

Chapter Fifteen

I worked with Jack throughout the afternoon. In the evening, I ate at the B&B, a simple meal of salad and quiche. The flannel-shirted men were there and Darla served all of us. I asked about Ian, and she told me he had to leave earlier in the day and she didn't know when he'd be back.

Her response didn't comfort me and I hoped that Ian hadn't gotten himself in trouble because of me. I liked him enough that I'd feel terrible if he had been fired and forced to leave the island.

I hurried to my room after, not sure what I would do, but I didn't want to stay out in a public area where I might have to engage with someone and say something I shouldn't.

I spent time that evening in one of the comfortable chairs near the side window, blinds closed, thinking about what to do. On the one hand, I liked a lot of the people I'd met. I liked the island. I really liked that I might have magic. On the other hand, I did not like Damien. I didn't like that I felt like people couldn't be honest about what they thought about him.

The ghost, Ann, had intimated that Damien had murdered her and others. She thought I might be in danger. I worried Ian might be in danger.

Still, I needed a job because my unemployment had run out and I was down to savings for the small expenses I had. I texted my sister, but she was at a school function with her kids and couldn't chat.

Instead, I took an early shower and went to bed, tossing and turning. When I finally fell asleep, I dreamed.

Fire lapped at a hallway I'd never seen, though I knew it was in the B&B. I ran from it, though in that way that one knows things in dreams, I knew I'd set the fire. I banged on doors as I went by. I heard people moving around inside, but no matter how long I pounded, no one came out.

I had to keep moving because the fire kept gaining on me as I tried to warn people. The hallway curved. I knew that around the corner, I'd find the stairs to the lower level.

Except when I turned, the lower level glowed with fire, too. Ian was struggling to climb the stairs and I pulled him up.

"I'm sorry," I said. "It's my fault."

Ian shook his head. He looked better than he had moments ago.

"I've never been trapped before," he said quietly, almost uncertain what he was saying.

"Have you been in a fire before?" It seemed strange.

Ian looked confused. "For a minute, I thought I had."

The flames roared down below but they didn't get any closer.

I didn't smell anything. I knew I had to be dreaming.

"And so you are," Damien said coming up behind me.

I whirled in the dream, my heart thundering in my chest. I tried to wake myself up, but I stayed in the B&B surrounded by flames. Even Ian was gone.

"Come with me," Damien said.

I didn't want to go with him in my dream any more than in real life. Yet, I couldn't stop myself. I followed him through the flames.

Instead of the B&B, I was in a cave. Bones lay on a stone in the cave. As I got closer, I noted the skull staring at me. The stone was darker beneath the bones than around the rest of it and I believed that as the body had lain there it decomposed slowly into the stone.

"You see her, don't you?" Damien asked.

I frowned, not certain what he meant. The skeleton was clearly there on the stone.

"She's there on the stone." I said. I knew as the words left my mouth that it was the wrong thing to say.

Damien's eyes darkened. He changed into a creature of smoke and oil, long tentacles of darkness reaching out to me. I felt the heat where one came close, but then my mom stood in front of me.

"Leave her alone!" Mom shouted. "You've taken enough from this family. Even the island is beginning to wake up to your evil!"

I tried to scream but couldn't. I couldn't even move, tangled in some sort of weed I couldn't quite make out. I struggled and fought and finally, I opened my eyes.

My room at the B&B surrounded me. The sheets were damp with sweat and I was tangled up in the blankets, a leg hanging off the side. The night felt too quiet and I reached to turn on the lamp but nothing happened.

I grabbed for my phone, wanting some level of light but it eluded my hands.

Someone banged on the door. I huddled in bed, in terror.

I heard a cat howl.

And then nothing. I sat frozen in bed, staring at the door, wanting to see what had happened to the cat but too terrified to move, half afraid of childhood monsters under the bed.

The door creaked open and the calico cat sauntered in as only cats could do. It leaped on the bed and rubbed against me.

"Wake up," it said.

I opened my eyes again to find myself lying in bed, on my back, no tossing or turning. This time when I reached out to turn on the lamp, fear rose through me that something worse would happen.

But the light went on, illuminating the room. The calico cat lay at the foot of my bed watching me with its large golden eyes. I stared at it for a long moment. Finally, it laid its head back down on its paws and went to sleep.

I settled back into the covers but left the light on. I dozed through the rest of the night, but I didn't get any real sleep.

Chapter Sixteen

I got up early and went out to have breakfast, which was served only half-heartedly by Darla. She said little to me and I said nothing to her. It was probably my imagination, but the food seemed less tasty without Ian around.

I wanted to ask where he was again, but didn't want to seem too eager. As I was finishing my breakfast, I realized that Darla had worked with Damien. She seemed to get along with him. Considering I had to study with him at least part of the day, I decided that next time she came out of the kitchen I'd ask her about her experiences when she first started seeing ghosts.

Naturally, she never reappeared.

Damien, however, did. I noticed that no one else was in the B&B for breakfast that morning, not even the flannel-shirted men who seemed to be fixtures around the place. The calico cat stuck her head out from under the writing desk while I went to the front room to study with Damien.

"I trust that the emergency session with Bernice allowed you to learn to meditate," he said.

"She gave me some pointers, yes," I agreed.

"Then there'll be no reason not to bring the ghost inside today." Damien said it like there was a mathematical precision to it.

I closed my eyes and focused on my breathing. I purposely did not focus on the ghost. I mean, I couldn't stop thinking about her, but only in the most general way. The dream remained solid in my mind though I tried not to focus on it. After a few minutes, I yawned.

"Does contacting the spirit world bore you so much?" Damien asked.

"No, but I had a nightmare last night and didn't get much sleep," I said.

I didn't open my eyes. I didn't want to see him watching me. I was back to being a child trying to make myself believe the monsters wouldn't see me if I didn't see them.

"And did your mother come rescue you?" Damien asked.

A chill went down my back. My eyes popped open. I realized I'd given away what was in my dream with that. "Is that common?" I asked. Maybe I could make it seem like I was just interested and not terrified of him.

"No."

"I have no idea why this ghost is so important to you, or why other people don't tell you to back off, but I'm tired of working on spirit magic. I have no idea why I can see that ghost or what it means or why it's so important to you, but I don't enjoy these lessons and I'm tired of being treated so disrespectfully," I said. I started to stand, my legs shaking.

I couldn't believe I'd just said that to anyone much less someone who terrified me. But really, being treated like a child was getting old. I could take being treated badly. I'd put up with it much of my adult life, but at least those people treated me like an adult nothing rather than a child nothing.

"Sit down," Damien said.

My legs threatened to obey, but I locked my knees. I moved around the side of the chair so I could rest my hand on the back to keep myself from falling.

Damien stood up. "Sit down or you will be banished from the island. From all enclaves, if I have any say. A mage who can't take orders or learn lessons from their betters is not safe for anyone."

"I'll go get my things," I said. Bernice and Sharon and the others had talked about other enclaves. I could find another place. Even if Damien was right and they wouldn't take me, better never learning to use my magic and remaining in the real world than staying there with him.

The calico cat came out from under the writing desk and stood in front of me, looking worried. I tried to step around her, but she mewed a little, almost as if she was trying to tell me something.

Damien waited behind me. There was no way I was going to slink back to him, yet I got the sense that the cat didn't want me to leave the island entirely. The indecision made me freeze.

"Come with me," Damien said. I felt the crawl of magic on my arms. My feet obeyed even though the rest of me didn't want to. The calico followed us as far as the door.

Outside the icy gray clouds hung low in the sky and a thick breeze quickly ate through my shirt, which was not meant for a day like that. My sweater was in my room, although the chill was deep enough that I doubted the sweater would have kept me warm.

I followed Damien out through the garden. I glanced back at the B&B and saw Darla watching me. The three cats from the garden followed at a distance, the gray one in the lead. I hoped that was a good sign.

Damien led me up the hill. I knew from talking to people that there was a condominium complex, the city activities center, and some homes. I had no idea what else lay that way. The hill was longer than I expected but I still reached the top far too soon. From there, the houses on the lake side disappeared and I had a glorious view. On a clear day, it seemed like I'd be able to see all the way to Michigan.

The other side of the hill was less steep than the one we'd just climbed up. A gentle slope led to a large well-maintained area of single-story condominiums on the inland side and on the lake side, a large park. Beyond a large square building that had to stand three or four stories held what appeared to be more condominiums.

Four cats peered out at us from under the bushes around the condos closest to us. Damien hurried by. A curtain twitched in one of the buildings. A patch of fog covered part of a window in another.

I heard the waves lapping quietly along the shoreline and wondered if there was a beach or if it was just a rocky coastline like it was below the accounting office. A low split rail fence lined the edge of the cliff in the well-maintained park with a single gate at the head of a path. It might be fun to walk on the beach, though I knew from growing up in Michigan that the lake was likely far too cold to swim in for most of the year. If there were shallows around, perhaps in late summer the cool water would feel good.

If I were taking a walk with someone, not being forced to follow Damien, I might have asked if the island had a swimming hole.

My feet moved slower than normal as I fought against Damien's control with every step. In my dream, my mother had come to rescue me. Too bad she was dead and could only help in dreams. I had little hope that anyone else on the island would help.

One of the cats, this one a large orange striped Tom, stepped out of the bushes and followed along behind us.

If I hadn't been in Damien's thrall, I'd have paused to rub its ears, but I had little control over my body. I could look where I wanted, but doing more than observing the sights was prevented.

I thought about picking up a rock or a stick or some-thing, but I couldn't bend down even as I continued moving. Damien didn't bother to turn around to make sure I followed. He knew I had to.

His magic tingled against my arms and the spell itself felt like a band around my chest. I imagined an old cowboy cartoon with a villain roped around the chest being dragged along behind a horse.

We passed by a large square building and then the trees and bushes began to take over more of the island. A small house, nothing more than a cottage, sat on the lakeside. While narrow lanes had branched off through the little complex of condos, the road we came to beyond the cottage was wider, more like the one we walked on. Cars could fit on these, easily, though I had yet to see even a golf cart.

Damien led me down that one, heading toward the inland area of the island. A few homes sat spread apart there, some up a slight incline looking down on their neighbors and others tucked into the embrace of the low hills. While there were plenty of bushes and flowers, I noted little grass.

The orange cat still followed, watching.

In the window of one house, I saw a giant skull laying on the window ledge, looking out at the world. I wondered if it was some sort of protective object or worse, if I was seeing another ghost. Then it raised itself up from the sofa where it laid and I realized it was a huge black and white dog. It barked at us. Only once.

Two black and white cats came out of a garden to watch us. One washed a paw, apparently uninterested in our walk. I wondered if the dog's bark had somehow called them. On an island where magic ruled—and I had no doubt there was some sort of magic at play given that I had no desire to go anywhere with this man—cats and dogs could probably communicate in ways I didn't understand.

Damien turned down a path that I almost missed. We walked long enough to leave the houses behind. A small but steep hill rose up and we started to climb. I'm in good shape, but my thighs burned. Even Damien slowed.

The path curved to the left and a set of five stone stairs greeted us. We climbed and at the last turn I was greeted by a huge house of glass and brick. The views had to be spectacular from each of the windows, either the main part of the island or out over the lake. Even frustrated and terrified, I couldn't help but admire the beauty of the place.

Damien entered through a set of black double doors. Inside, the narrow board wood floors looked as old as the B&B. The furnishings were all pristine antique pieces, the wood shiny and bright. Unlike the antique stores my middle sister loved to frequent, there weren't too many of the items crowded in a space. This was a room meant to be lived in, or would have been had any of the pieces actually looked comfortable.

Floral patterns adorned the upholstery. And while thick, plush, beautifully colored Persian-style rugs adorned the floors, the walls had been painted plain beige at some point.

"Sit," Damien ordered.

I sat on the nearest sofa. The spindly legs didn't look sturdy enough to hold me, but the wood was solid. While the seat and back were upholstered, the cushioning left much to be desired. If I had ever loved antiques, I lost any fondness for them right then.

"Close your eyes," Damien ordered. I felt the tingling on my arms get stronger.

I did as I was told, though I hated it.

"You will focus on the ghost and bring her here," he snapped.

I pushed against the compulsion to think about her. I expended the same sort of effort to push him out of my head that I might have used to hold the door against an intruder. Every muscle in my body tensed and I fought the compulsion with everything I had.

I heard a noise outside, but I continued my fight, hoping against hope that the sound was Xavier and perhaps the big guy from the police station coming to rescue me. Once that was done, I'd leave the island and go back to my life or perhaps someone could tell me about another enclave. I had a feeling that Damien would continue his rule on this island.

So many wonderful people on the island and such a sweet place. I couldn't fathom why the people didn't get together and stand up to him.

Those thoughts kept his compulsion at bay.

I heard the screech of a cat and the crash and thud of something against the house. I felt the vibration through my feet.

The pressure of Damien's mind released me.

My eyes flew open.

What seemed like a hundred cats, several dozen dogs,

including the large black and white dog I'd noticed earlier, a half dozen goats, pigs, and sheep all came rushing in.

I moved off the sofa and tried to run to the door, but animals crowded in, leaving no space for me. A towering black horse with eyes rolling around in rage or fear leaped into the room, hooves thundering against the wood floor, his entire focus on Damien.

I pressed myself back against a side wall, hoping none of the animals would harm me. I rubbed my arms, only then realizing the tingling had stopped.

If there was a spell on the animals, it wasn't being cast by anyone nearby.

I glanced over in time to see a dozen skeletal bodies shambling into the room. One of them turned their skull towards me, the blank black eyes staring in my direction. Terror filled me at being noticed.

I looked around for a place to run, but with the room filled with animals, I had no place to go.

Chapter Seventeen

My knees shook. The cats and goats and a particularly fat sheep made way for the skeletal creature. The one focused on me came towards me while the others surrounded Damien,

"Go," it whispered, pointing a bony finger towards the door it had come through.

I stepped that direction, worried about hurting one of the cats that had gathered in the room, but they quickly scampered out of my way. Several sat on top of a china hutch like vultures and two others sat on the back of the large black and white dog.

I didn't need to be told twice and upon figuring out that I could scamper through the mob of creatures, I hurried out the door.

The calico cat from the B&B waited for me on the outside steps. Upon seeing me, she started to purr. I glanced back, then hurried along down the stairs. She ran in front of me, leading me away from the house.

I followed.

She led me down the path that Damien had taken me,

but instead of going back out to the street she ducked under a bush and ran through there. I hesitated. I didn't hear anything behind me, but it would be easy enough for Damien to follow me. Heck, with his magic, he could probably find me anywhere on the island.

I ducked around the bush, hoping I didn't damage it too much. Leaves I'd pushed aside popped back into place as I turned back, looking to see how obvious my trail was.

The calico cat waited for me on the other side of the bush.

She hurried down a narrow trail, more akin to an animal track than anything used by humans. Low plants covered parts of the path and then large holes would show up in the middle, some filled with water. Branches struck my face as I forced my way through the brush.

The cat moved easily. She hopped over the puddles and holes. She sat in front of one particularly deep and large hole that looked as if the ground had caved in and waited to be sure I noticed. It was wide enough that I didn't think she could leap over it and I expected her to go around, but she pushed off the ground with her hind legs and landed easily on the far side.

She looked back at me, waiting.

I wasn't sure I could leap it so I pushed into the bushes and went around the edge, looking down. Water stood in places at the bottom and it was probably five feet deep. I wasn't likely to die from such a fall, but I could have been badly hurt if I hadn't seen it. Of course, I wasn't moving that fast, but it was nice of the calico to care.

I shivered against the breeze that came up. I hated that I didn't even have a sweater. Large drops of rain started to fall. If I'd run to the main road, I could probably have found a place to shelter. Now, I could freeze to death.

The cat hurried along, her fur twitching as fat drops hit her back. She clearly liked the rain as little as I did.

The path curved. She darted to a large tree with branches widely spaced over low scrub. The scrub had been trampled and worked by feet for a long time. In the distance I noticed split rail fences. We were on the edge of a farm, probably one where the animals got out from time to time.

The cat slipped around the side of the tree and disappeared.

I looked up, thinking she'd leapt up to one of the branches, but nothing. As I stood there, turning in all directions, wondering where she could have disappeared, I heard the faintest mew.

It came from a crack in the wood of the tree, so narrow I barely noticed it. I couldn't believe the cat had slipped in there. I certainly couldn't.

The crack widened as if the tree was opening a door for me. When the opening was wide enough, I slipped inside. It was either that or hope that the fields eventually led to a house where they'd take me in and warm me up.

And be willing to lie to Damien.

As the tree closed itself off, I worried I'd get claustrophobic or be squashed but no such thing happened. Instead, I was able to sink down with my knees up against my chest and rest. It wasn't super comfortable but not nearly as bad as I had feared. The calico sat on my feet.

Her body heat warmed me. I couldn't believe such a tiny cat put off so much heat, but I soon stopped shivering. At least from the cold.

I needed help and I didn't know where to get it. I didn't have my phone or my purse, which might have been a good thing because then I couldn't be tracked. It seemed like the animals on the island were protecting me. The calico, now rescuing me, had seemed to want to keep me from my room. Perhaps this was preferable to what would've happened had I made it to my room.

I closed my eyes and focused on the ghost. I got colder than ever.

Ann stood before me, not in her skeletal visage but as a girl. She seemed to seep through the wood of the tree and looked at me.

"You're safe enough here. Let the island know when you're in danger and it will do what it can to protect you. I've made myself known to it and let it know that Damien has harmed me. The island can't untangle itself from him by itself, but it can fight back, much as you did when you fought to keep from focusing on me at his house," Ann said.

"What do I do next? Who can I trust?" I asked. "Can I go back to the B&B?"

"Darla's at the B&B, so I wouldn't go there. She's loyal to Damien," Ann said.

"Why would anyone be loyal to him?" I snapped. Probably louder than I should have but it seemed ridiculous to me that anyone would voluntarily be loyal to Damien.

"She has spirit magic and so does he. Bernice started training her and pushed her to see ghosts, something that terrified Darla. Damien came in and protected her and told her it was okay to be afraid. If she's too afraid to use her magic, it doesn't challenge him. I also sense that he linked to her in some way so he can use her magic," Ann replied.

"Can I go stay with someone else? Maybe at the accounting office, even? It's not particularly comfortable here. If the island knows..."

"We have to stop him. It's gone on long enough. The people here are cowed. The island does so much for them, but then there's Damien. They put up with him because mostly he leaves people alone. Unfortunately, he heard you talked to me. That was my mistake. I was so shocked that anyone could hear me!" Ann shook her head.

"How?" I asked.

"When it stops raining, you will be led to my bones. Removing them will help break the connection. I was the first. You'll need magic, though."

"The other islanders…" I started.

"I'm not sure who would be willing to stand up to him," Ann cut me off. "Even those who should be able to do not seem to understand their own power. Rest now. The rain will fall for some time and even then it won't be terribly warm. You'll be safe here."

I let my eyes close. The drum of rain lulled me into a light sleep. If I'd been able to stretch out, I suspect it would have been one of the most wonderful sleeps I'd ever had, but unfortunately, I was tucked into the trunk of a tree, somehow.

When I woke, the rain had stopped. I stood. The calico glared at me but made no move to leave. I couldn't figure out how to get out of the tree on my own so I stretched as well as I could and settled back in.

It occurred to me to wonder if anyone missed me. Bernice would have come by the B&B for my lesson later in the morning. Jack would have expected me at the accounting office. Sharon knew that Damien was supposed to train me. I couldn't count on anyone searching for me or being worried about me, not unless Darla said something.

The calico cat finally stood and stretched. It put out a paw along one side of the tree and an opening appeared. It grew large enough for me to slip out, which I did.

It was dark, and the night was cold.

The cat hurried along a trail away from Damien's. I

followed once again, already shivering. If only Damien had allowed me to grab a sweater before we left, but at least it was just a general chill. No wind whipped at my body to steal what heat I generated. And, sometime during my stay in the tree my clothing had dried.

The trail led towards the split rail fence that made me think about a farm. The calico cat skirted the edges of it and then picked up another trail that led across the island away from where I knew the town was. I'd been charged with finding Ann's bones. I had to trust that the calico cat.

A low breeze blew through, the first one that I'd felt, but fortunately it was gentle enough to bring only a bit more chill—either that or I was so cold that a breeze couldn't bring more. I smelled the stink of manure and wondered which of the animals that had pushed their way into Damien's house lived on this farm.

Then I wondered if the animals often just took off on errands of their own and how their owners felt about that.

I hurried along after the calico who wasn't pausing to sniff or stalk like a normal cat but rather pranced down the trail like someone on a mission. Of course, the cat *was* on a mission.

We got closer to the shore and I heard the sound of the water lapping at the edge of the island. I couldn't see the lake, not only because of how dark it was, though the stars and the nearly full moon did a decent enough job lighting the way, but because the land rose in a ridge. When I reached the top, I looked down at a narrow stretch of beach. This ridge was only a few feet high, low enough that I'd have no problem jumping from the top but the cat had found another trail and was already halfway down, not taking in the view.

I followed. The scrub that had clung to the top stopped abruptly about halfway down the short trail. The water at high tide might reach that high. I hoped that if the tide started coming in, I'd have time to get up to the ridge above it. There was no way I could survive the chill of Lake Michigan in fall.

The calico cat sauntered down the beach. It was colder near the water and my body was no longer shivering, but actively shaking. My arms were crossed across my chest, hoping to keep in some little bit of heat, but I doubted I was making much difference.

I watched as the cat slipped into a cave and then peeked out at me. I hurried to follow. At least there, any breeze that drifted in off the water wouldn't hit me so hard. The rocks nearest the beach were dark, damp. At least the water wasn't lapping at my feet—not yet, anyway.

Once I followed the cat inside, it hurried off into the dark. I couldn't see a thing.

I moved slowly. It turned, its bright eyes shining enough for me to see their glow. She seemed to cock her head to one side and then a little ball of light appeared at the tip of her tail and she hurried across the cave. The ceiling was low and I had to duck my head in places, but at least the light at the tip of the cat's tail was bright enough for me to see where I had to bend down.

The cavern narrowed into a tunnel, but the cat kept going. Fortunately, the ceiling was high enough and the tunnel wide enough for me to follow fairly easily. The cat was jogging quickly and I had to work to keep the light on her tail in sight.

We came to another cavern. I noted the floor in there was dustier. A few stalagmites rose up around me. The calico cat moved easily around them. They were so close together that I had to turn sideways to get between them.

Fortunately, the cat waited for me at another tunnel opening. She hurried inside. At first, the ground raised just enough for my thighs to feel the incline. Then it angled to my right, almost back the way we came. By the time the tunnel led downward, far more steeply than the slight upward incline, I was completely lost, knowing only that I was heading down into the bowels of the island.

At least it wasn't so cold in the caverns. It wasn't warm, not like the tree trunk, but while the air was cool, the chill wouldn't have been uncomfortable if I hadn't gotten so cold crossing the island. Moving helped keep me warm, though, and I hadn't started to sweat.

Finally, we came to a huge cavern. Stalactites hung down from the ceiling. A few stalagmites had begun to grow, but something or someone had lopped them off. A fat one sat in the middle of the cavern. The calico cat stopped near it.

Dread filled my stomach as I walked closer to it. I was reminded of a dais upon which a speaker might stand. I had seen this before. In my dream.

I shuddered. Fear filling my body. This was the place I had dreamed of.

I knew, before reaching it that I would see bones upon the broken stalagmite. Getting closer, I was right. Even the small threads of clothing were there and the darkening on the stone from when the body had rotted away.

I had found Ann.

Chapter Eighteen

I stared at the bones for some time. I'd dreamed about them, yes, but I'd not seen them. In fact, I'd never seen a human skeleton before, other than in the visions of the ghost, and, of course, on television. My breathing hitched a little as I realized what I was looking at.

For the first few moments, nothing had seemed real. Now, though, the bones were all too real. This had been a person. A woman named Ann. If my dreams were as correct about her identity as they had been about where she was, she was my great aunt on my mother's side.

The idea of finding her bones had seemed impossible. It was a quest that I'd turned over to Xavier as police chief, but here I was, standing in front of them, having found them.

"What do I do?" I murmured.

The earth of the cavern remained silent around me.

"Burn them," Ann said, appearing beside me. "Use the intent of the fire to burn the ties that I have to the island by my blood and bodily fluids leaching into the stone. Burn the very stone. You're strong enough."

Fire was easy, at least. And other than the bones, there didn't appear to be anything in the cavern to burn. The calico cat sat off to the side, washing her paw.

I closed my eyes focusing on the warmth in my belly. I let it flow upward. I pictured the bones burning. I picture a hot fire, one that would be hot enough to burn down through the stone.

I let it go when I could stand it no more.

A huge flame whooshed up from the bones, reaching to the ceiling of the cavern. The heat was intense and I had to take several steps backwards. Even then, sweat beaded my brow. The calico looked at it, sniffing. It stepped back a few feet as well.

As the bones burned, I continued to back up until a wall blocked any further progress. Even then, I felt uncomfortably warm.

I noticed the calico cat appeared unaffected by the heat. She sat just far enough away that she didn't need worry about her fur getting singed. Her golden eyes watched the flames intently.

The flames finally started to burn low enough that I felt merely hot and not about to burst into flames myself. The calico gave me a long look when I shifted my weight, but she stayed where she was, eyes watching the dying fire.

It seemed like it took forever for the fire to go completely out. I wiped sweat from my forehead with a hand that was already slick. My clothing was so wet, I'd probably freeze when I went outside. I hoped I'd done what Ann needed me to do.

"Now you need to head further into the caverns," Ann said, almost as if she heard my thoughts. Maybe she did.

I looked for another tunnel but didn't immediately see one. The calico cat hurried towards the left and slipped through a crack that seemed far too narrow for me.

However, the walls moved slightly and I was able to turn sideways and squeeze through.

I slid in between the rock and hoped that the island wouldn't push the walls closer together. Before, it had seemed to create spaces more than large enough but not this time. A stray stone gouged my back. I felt something scrape my knee. I remained sideways and took a single step to my left.

I felt something gouge at my thigh and heard a rip. I was wearing my nice new jeans and now they were probably torn. I'd have to purchase more if I got out of there. Or perhaps David could magically fix them, though I wasn't holding out too much hope. I kept shuffling one step at a time to my left, hoping that the narrow passage would end. I could still see the light on the end of the calico's tail and I headed towards it, though I wished I were a cat to slip through places like this so easily.

After a half dozen steps with still no end in sight, I started to feel panicked about where I was. I worried the passage was getting too narrow and I would be trapped there. Even if the island didn't do it, it was certainly possible someone like Damien could trap me there. Even without being linked to the island, it seemed like he'd be powerful, though what did I know?

"Keep going," Ann whispered to me. "I can't stay visible much longer without my body to anchor me."

I took another step. And then another.

Finally, the passage seemed to open up enough that I could breathe. I couldn't quite face forward but I wasn't pressed between two walls.

I moved faster and more easily. My breathing was deeper too. My heart rate continued to stay high, but of course, I was still terrified.

"Hurry. He's coming and we need to close off this passage," Ann said.

I moved as quickly as I could through the narrow passage until it opened into a small alcove. The calico cat sat there, its tail high with the light on the tip, waiting and watching. As soon as I cleared the passage, the walls slid together, just a few inches. I'd have been able to make it through this passage but not the earlier one.

The calico hurried across the little chamber to another passage with a floor that sloped down. It was wide, but not high.

Soon enough I had to get down on my knees and crawl. Fortunately, my feline friend slowed down when that happened, perhaps anticipating that I wasn't used to walking on all fours. She hadn't slowed down in the other passage, leaving me with only dim light, so I appreciated this thoughtfulness.

It was hard crawling when the passage sloped down at a steep angle. I'd have liked to have gone backwards but there was no way to turn around. I had to keep going. Fortunately, that was the only place that made me that uncomfortable and after a short crawl, the ceiling started to raise again.

I came to what might have been either a wide passage or a cavern. A few stalactites hung from the ceiling and I had to duck under them and four stalagmites stood sentry near the right hand wall. The passage was wide enough that there was plenty of room for me to move.

I was cooling off from the fire earlier, but while hurrying through the passages, I had felt comfortable. Now I was cold, probably thanks to my wet clothing. Movement helped but with sweat that had dampened my jeans and shirt there wasn't a lot I could do to warm up, not unless I set another fire and I didn't trust my ability to keep it under control. Not that there was much to burn there beneath the earth.

The passage narrowed and a few steps later I came to a junction of three different passages. The calico took the one on the right that sloped down some more. It ended in a small chamber. This one didn't appear used at all. In the dim light the brown floor looked smooth and unused, not a speck of the dry dirt moved. A couple of rocks glowed red and I stayed away from them.

The calico, however, moved closer to a pair of them and stretched out.

"It's okay," Ann said. "The glowing rocks are warming. You need to dry off."

I moved over to one particularly large one and settled against it.

"How long do I have to stay here?" I asked.

"Damien's power needs to bleed off a bit. A few of the spells on certain townspeople will fail. You'll get help then. The linking spell has been broken so he won't be able to acquire more power unless he holds a new sacrifice at the full moon. He'll need a new witch, one who isn't very attuned to the island," Ann said. "The more untapped power, the better. In all likelihood he'll come looking for you."

Great. I was stuck in a cavern until Damien's power weakened and then he'd probably come after me to try and sacrifice me to regain that power. I had a feeling that if he did that, he'd take great pleasure in finally destroying me.

I shivered, although the rocks warmed me and my clothing was already starting to dry. They hadn't been soaking, just damp enough to keep my body heat from maintaining my warmth. The heat from the glowing stones helped, although now everything I wore was stiff and stinky.

The calico cat curled up and went back to sleep. Although it didn't seem that long ago that I'd woken up after a brief nap in the tree trunk, I realized I was tired from the exertion. And hungry. I'd barely been able to stand the first few times I'd raised magic and yet this time, I'd been able to hurry through the tunnels and the caverns and hardly noticed anything all.

Holding up a hand, I realized it was shaking just a bit.

"Holly!" Damien called. It echoed around me.

I scrunched back in the corner.

The calico's ear twitched but she didn't move. I tried to be as confident as the cat, but Damien calling my name kept me from anything close to relaxation. The cat seemed aware of things going on in the caverns, seemed to believe that Damien couldn't get to me, but I worried that he knew so much more than I did. I kept envisioning him finding a way into these tunnels and my little hidden cave.

Finally, the calling disappeared and I dosed for a while, dreaming of food and of feeling better. When I woke up, the calico was having a bath. I tried to stand but my legs felt weak. Maybe the adrenaline of burning Ann's body had kept me going and now I was paying for it. Everything felt shaky.

I needed to get out of the cavern. I needed food. The calico stretched and cocked her head. She trotted over to me and let me rub her head, though my hands were shaking. When she moved, I tried to stand but my legs were weak and my stomach felt as if it were falling down through my body and out my feet.

Dark spots danced in front of my eyes. If I hadn't been leaning against the wall, I'd have fallen. I sank back down into a crouch. The calico went back to having a bath and didn't seem to care that I might be dying.

Chapter Nineteen

I waited in the tunnels for quite some time. I dozed off and on, not sure how long I was unconscious during any one doze. It wasn't as if I had my phone or any way of telling time. Given that I'd spent the night in the tree, I knew that at least a day had passed.

My mouth felt dry and parched. When that became uncomfortable, water started trickling down the wall not far from me, landing in a stone that was conveniently shaped like a bowl. I hadn't noticed the bowl earlier so I had a feeling the island had realized I needed water.

I crawled over to it and cupped it to my hands, drinking, feeling the coolness go down my throat. It helped, but my stomach still needed food.

I tried to stand again, to make my way out, hopefully to find help, but my legs weren't cooperating.

At some point the calico's ears flicked and she hurried out of the cavern. I tried to follow but couldn't make myself move. When she was well into the passage, the light from her tail flickered out leaving me with only the glowing red stones that cast shadows like dripping blood from the walls of the cavern.

If Damien found me because I couldn't move, that blood would be mine. I was so tired and weak that I found it difficult to care.

When I heard footsteps hurrying along the passage, I became resigned to my life being over.

I felt badly that my sisters would miss me. Worse, it wasn't likely that they'd know what happened to me. Chances were, I'd be a missing person. I hoped that they'd find a way to make their peace with that.

My nieces and nephews would miss the aunt who always played with them and could be counted on to help them put even their craziest ideas in motion. I'd miss helping them. And I'd miss their weddings, if they had them, and their children, if they had families. I'd miss their adult triumphs and I wouldn't be there to comfort them in their sorrows. My heart hurt at the thought.

While I might be able to do one last bit of magic, I had a feeling that might wipe me out. Easier to let Damien kill me right there.

The footsteps sounded closer. I dry swallowed, realizing I needed water again. If I weren't too afraid to move, I would have leaned forward to dip my hands in the bowl of water next to me. I might hurt and I might be tired, but deep down I realized I didn't want to die.

A few tears leaked from my eyes thinking about the people I loved most and the things I wished I had done differently. If only I hadn't answered that stupid ad or if I had, if only I had let Damien frighten me away from the island.

A shadow reached the cavern. I breathed out when I realized it was a cat. This one, when it appeared, was a solid black with orange eyes. In the red light that danced in the cavern, this cat's eyes looked like tiny flames.

It mewed and ran over to me, rubbing its head against my legs. I reached down to rub its ears and it began to purr. The calico followed it. She no longer had a light at the tip of her tail. She sat down in her spot. After a few seconds, she laid down, tucking her paws beneath her chest. Her ears were forward and she was alert.

Another shadow, a taller one, more human-like reached the cavern. This couldn't be Damien. The cats were too relaxed. Still, my breath hitched and I realized I couldn't make myself take a full breath. My heart hammered in my ears so loudly I couldn't hear the black cat purr nor could I hear any more footsteps.

I gasped when Ian rounded the corner into the cavern. He had a flashlight with him and a backpack.

"There you are," he said. "Darla insisted you had left the island, but the cats were going crazy."

"Damien forced me to follow him, but then…" I trailed off, not sure how to tell the story. I reached over to drink from the bowl next to me.

Ian squatted and set the pack down. He pulled out a large bottle of water and handed it to me. Then he pulled out a thermos.

"I made some of the tea," he said. My arms tingled as he waved a hand over it.

I recapped the water bottle and took the thermos gratefully. The first sip of tea from the tiny cup was the most wonderful thing I'd ever tasted. I'd be back at the B&B on a regular basis just for it so I could remember the sensation. My body's weaknesses didn't so much ease as they smoothed themselves out. Muscles that I hadn't realized were tight relaxed and softened.

I groaned in pleasure.

"So tell me what happened," Ian said. He was cross legged on the floor of the cave. He handed me piece of cheese with a cracker to munch on.

I told him how Damien had come by and when I refused to be treated like a child, how he'd put a spell on me and forced me out of the B&B. I told him how I'd been thinking about leaving the island to get away from Damien because I felt threatened by him.

I talked about being at his house and being rescued by the animals on the island.

"The cats are magic, aren't they?" I asked, looking at him.

"They are," Ian said. "All the animals are, except those brought by people living here. The horse is strong. It's been on the island as long as anyone can remember, but it never changes. If there's a living heart of the island, I expect that's it."

The cracker tasted good. I wanted more, but I settled for sipping the tea.

Ian brought out some sliced apple. The sugars in the fruit were divine. I felt my spine straightening as I ate. My stomach was still demanding something more solid, but this would work. I continued to sip at the tea.

I told Ian about hiding in the tree trunk with the calico cat. Then about following her to the caverns where I had found the skeleton and burned it.

"I felt something change about twelve hours ago," Ian said nodding. "I bet that was it. It was like my magic suddenly became clearer, easier to access."

"So do you think that Damien was siphoning magic from everyone on the island?" I asked.

Ian shrugged. "I don't worry about how things work so long as I get paid to hang out at the B&B. I love being one of the first people anyone meets on the island, and everyone always comes back some mornings so I always know what's going on. I mean, I'm a gossip at the best of times. Can you image what a dream job that was?!" Ian laughed at himself as if we were just having a picnic in a cavern beneath the earth.

Ian might not worry about it, but I did. If Damien were still able to link to others and siphon their magic, that might make him powerful enough to find another sacrifice at the full moon.

"Ann Rodgers, the ghost, sent me to burn her bones. She said if Damien finds another sacrifice, someone the island isn't attuned to, he can re-set the same spell again," I said. "It sounded like he had some people spelled to listen to him."

"The entire island was spelled to listen to him," Ian said. "It's why no one spoke out even though just about everyone was scared to death of him. If you tried, you got sick, like I did the other day, and I'm more resistant than most."

Suddenly more pieces of the puzzle came together.

I sipped more tea.

"Ann says I need to stop him, but I'm not sure how."

"If you turn up, he'll know," Ian said, suddenly serious. "While he might not have everyone under his thumb, he has a few people that he's helped that feel loyal to him and they'd let him know where you were."

"I can't stay here the entire time," I said.

"It isn't terribly pleasant," Ian agreed looking around. "At least it's warm though."

"Ann said I might be his preferred sacrifice. But it seems like the island is helping me?"

"Just because he wants to make you a sacrifice, doesn't mean he can. And if he gets someone else this time, he can probably force the island to let him take you another time.

It protects us, but Damien has been bending those rules a long time. Sharon says it started before she came, but I've heard a few old-timers say it got worse when she arrived. Damien taught her how to use magic."

I hated that Sharon might be part of whatever it was that Damien was doing to the island. I liked her and she'd seemed nice.

"He did it because he probably sensed leadership in her," Ian went on. "If he gets the leaders to follow, then no one reports him to the U Council. They look into anything unusual at any of the enclaves. Once or twice a year one of them comes to visit. Damien always leaves the island around that time so they can't ask to speak to him."

"He hides from them?" I asked.

"He avoids them. My guess is that they might sense that his connection to the island isn't a normal connection and that might trigger a real investigation."

I finished my tea and Ian brought out more food. My stomach rejoiced. I stretched out my legs and moved around, working out the kinks that had set in. My hair felt lank and my clothing reeked, but I now felt like I had the energy to do something about those things should the opportunity arise.

"I don't know what I need to do next," I said. "Ann told me to avoid him but it seemed like I had to do something before the full moon."

Ian closed his eyes, looking thoughtful. The calico cat joined him. The black cat padded around the cavern sniffing at all the nooks and crannies as if looking for a treat someone had missed. It had made it nearly around the cavern when Ian opened his eyes.

"I've gone through all the spells I know and I don't have a clue how to stop someone like Damien. I mean, burning him would work, but he'd probably just put out the flames with his own magic. I could try and bury him in the earth, but again, he could move the earth so that he wasn't buried."

"What about poison or something like that?" I asked.

"At this point, I can only think he'd be expecting it. Besides, if we actually kill him, we have to live with that, always assuming the island lets us, though it might, considering all he's done. And Xavier would have to investigate, and he takes his job very seriously. Between you and me, I think his pride in being a police officer is the reason he's here. He wasn't well-treated by the police and his family aren't exactly police-friendly, if you know what I mean. Anyway, the more pride he takes, the more power he gets so he's got all sorts of reasons not to look the other way," Ian said.

"I thought Sharon said we don't talk about what fuels our magic?"

"Mostly we don't. But I have a hunch about these things. And sometimes Kate, one of our residents, has a moment where she starts berating someone for something. It's usually related to whatever shame fuels their magic. I think her power is the island's way of challenging people when they get here."

I thought about Ian's comments. Interesting how the island would challenge people. "Has anyone ever lost their magic after a challenge?" I asked.

"Now and then someone just leaves after Katie has an episode. We call them spells although it's not like she puts a hex on someone. She just has a moment where she's not fully there. And sometimes people suddenly have an influx of magic, but like I said, others leave. I don't know if they leave because they lose their magic or if they just don't want to have to go through that again." Ian gave a shrug.

"Has Katie ever had an episode around Damien?" I asked. Maybe he had a weakness in his area of shame.

Ian laughed out loud at that. "I can't imagine he'd have let her live. I don't know what shames him unless it's not having enough power."

The black cat came over and meowed at Ian and put a paw on his lap. Ian rubbed his ears.

Behind him, a shadow rose up, shaped vaguely like a huge cat but a huge cat a five year old had drawn.

"Ian…" I whispered.

Ian looked behind him.

"Hey!" His voice had a tone like he recognized an old friend.

"Damien never had power like that," a voice said.

"How did he end up here?" Ian asked.

"He was obsessed with a woman who came here. He was holding hands with her when she left the ferry for the island. Normally, the clasped hands would break apart but he wouldn't allow it. As always, he was taught but he could do only the smallest of spells. On the second day, he took the woman to a cave and murdered her."

"Ann Rodgers," I said.

"Yes." The shadow faded.

"That was Socrates," Ian said, continuing to rub his ears. "A cat can't speak so he creates a shadow to speak with us when he has something to say."

"These cats really are magic, aren't they?" I said.

"Aren't all cats?" Ian returned with his trademark grin. "I think all of nature is magic. It's just more so here. Or maybe we're more used to seeing it. I see things in the trees when I go to visit my sister and her husband that I never noticed before. I see signs in the birds flying overhead and I can always, always predict the weather around their house."

"I hope I live long enough to be able to visit my sisters. We still don't know how to destroy Damien. Now that would have been useful, to be told how to do that," I said.

"If Socrates knew and needed us to know, he would have told us," Ian said.

"Did he come with that name or did you name him?" I reached out a hand to the black cat. He sniffed at it and allowed me to lightly rub his ears.

"I named him. I guess a few other people have named the cats but mostly they're just the calico, the gray, the tiger cat, the huge cat, and so on."

"I don't think I've seen the huge cat," I said.

"You'd know if you did," Ian said. "I'm surprised he didn't go to Damien's to rescue you. Of course, he's kind of a big love bug, so he probably held back."

"There was a big dog that helped out, but I saw him in a house," I started.

Ian nodded. "When you live here a little longer, you'll get it. The animals pick a mage and live with them if they want to. The Harlequin Great Dane lives with Carl. You might have met him when you saw Xavier. Big guy. He adores that dog. And one of the gray cats. I think he calls the dog Mutt and the cat Jeff."

I chuckled a little at the old-time reference. My dad had talked about Mutt and Jeff. A pang hit me, missing him, suddenly. I wanted to know what he'd say about the island. Further, I wanted to know what secret shames might have kept him from getting to the island. As I thought about it, I realized how little I actually knew about my father.

I didn't have time to wander too far down memory lane. I needed to figure out how to stop Damien.

"If he's off the island, would he still have magic?" I asked.

"When he's been linked to the island, yes," Ian said. "He leaves now and again and I can't imagine that he'd do so if he didn't have magic. I think that maybe burning the bones of Ann, who was probably the woman he robbed of magic when he first got here, probably keeps him retaining whatever magic he has. I expect that there was something in the spell that he figured out or created or willed into existence that allowed him to use what magic she had even though she was dead. Now the bones are gone, so it's only what he's set up to siphon off people and those spells are dying."

"He's leaking magic," I said. "He'll get weaker."

"But tonight is the full moon when he can make another sacrifice."

"Everyone except me is linked to the island through their magic. It won't let him hurt anyone," I said.

"Given what you've been through and the island coming to your aid, I suspect it won't let him hurt you either," Ian said. "Ann was your ancestor, right?"

I nodded.

"She told the island who you were and it would have been her influence that protected you earlier. Damien wouldn't have expected that. He'll probably still expect that you're not linked and he can murder you, but I think the island will keep that from happening."

"Do you think I should allow him to find me?" I asked. "It would keep someone from off-island safe."

Ann appeared. She was less formed, like a fading picture. "He's off the island already. He said he'd been harsh with you and is hoping to bring you back. He's going to find someone to sacrifice."

"Will he use the same room for this sacrifice?" I asked.

Ian shivered as he frowned at me, though I saw something dawn in his eyes. He knew I was talking to a ghost.

"He can do it wherever," Ann said. "He just makes a circle and calls some magic. He has enough left to do it. I'm not strong enough to influence the island."

"We can get Xavier and Carl to search for Damien," I said to Ian when Ann had disappeared again. I shivered from the cold that had settled over my body, though Ian looked as if he was already warming up.

Ian shook his head. "I tried to get them to look for you, but Xavier didn't remember who you were. I think Damien put a forgetting spell on them. That's an easier spell than linking and influencing the way he was so it will take longer to wear off. You'd have to go re-introduce yourself and get him to believe you."

"What about you?" I asked.

Ian shrugged. "No one takes me seriously here. And I've been known to try and prank Damien before so they'll think it's another prank."

"But if you were saying he'd murder someone..." I suggested. I needed to focus, though I wondered why Ian could remember me.

Ian shook his head. "Everyone knows the island protects people. I'm not sure anyone else has ever tried to bring someone to the island that didn't have magic, not until long after they'd lived on the island and the island understood their longing for their loved ones. Sharon is certain it can't be done. Maybe it can't, but if Damien can find someone with a low level of magic and not introduce them to the island..."

I nodded. We had to do something to stop him.

Chapter Twenty

Having eaten and had plenty to drink, I felt better. The cavern was warm and rather cozy with both me and Ian sitting there. The calico cat was curled up, her head on her paws in front of one of the glowing stones. There were fewer of them than there had been, almost as if the island knew what temperature would work for us.

In addition to food, Ian had brought a light blanket.

"It would have looked weird for me to be going out on a picnic alone," he said. "Darla was nosing around so I didn't go into your room, but I did grab this lap blanket which will help keep you a little warmer."

"You'd think that because I have a room, people would remember I'm in the B&B," I said.

"I suspect that's why Damien's spell didn't work on me. I'm linked to the B&B. I always know when someone goes in or out and who's on the island. Sometimes I can tell if they're really upset or really, really happy. It's like that attachment allows me to know what people need. It happens at the restaurant, too. David says it sort of happens at the clothing store. He'll have this moment where he needs to order a certain type of top or pants and about the time it arrives, someone needs it. He doesn't always get it, but he's good," Ian said.

"If I live and I stay on the island, will that happen to me with the accounting office?" I asked.

Ian laughed. "You'd think, right? I don't know. Jack is kind of a hoarder and he's super compulsive about organization so you've always got so much stuff there, I doubt you'll ever have to special order anything. It's not like magic can do taxes—which if you think about it is really way too bad. That's something you could package and sell."

I chuckled a little with him, but I was still focused on what we might do about Damien.

"I still don't know what we can do about Damien. I mean, I guess I could go back to the B&B if he's not even on the island."

"He'll be back later though," Ian said. "I don't know where he'll do the sacrifice. On the one hand, he'll like the cavern because that's where he got his power originally. Something had to lead him there, some sense or other. But he also knows you've found it and would easily find it again and the island isn't likely to let him murder you, not now."

We both stood up. Socrates and the little calico trotted out through the tunnel. I went next and Ian came last. When we came to the next room, the one before the narrow passage, the cats paused and looked at Ian.

He closed his eyes and I felt my arms tingle. Then an elevator appeared.

My mouth dropped open.

"Oh, *come on*," Ian said. "You don't think I wandered through tunnels for hours trying to find you. Yuck."

He pressed a button and the silver metal doors swooshed open and we got on. Inside, the walls were shiny black with chrome handrails. The floor was dark wood. Mirrors covered the ceiling. It even smelled like a hotel elevator, those scents of fresh laundry and human sweat mixing and mingling into that indefinable whole.

I felt the movement as the elevator raced up. It rose every bit as fast as the super-speed elevators on the tallest high rises I'd visited. Moments later it stopped with hardly any sense of drop and the doors slid open.

Both Ian and I stepped out. He did something with his hand which made my arms tingle again and the elevator was gone.

I looked around. We were in a field surrounded by a low split rail fence painted white. This wasn't the field I'd seen when I'd followed the calico across the island. She sat near me and was watching the two of us. Socrates had trotted off towards a gambrel-roofed barn in worn wood.

"Where are we?" I asked.

"We're nearly at the center of the island. I expect the big cavern was as close as Damien could get to the center. He probably figured that would be a place of power. He wasn't wrong. He was just wrong about the land being the only thing that held power around here," Ian said.

The big black stallion appeared in the field. I didn't know how I hadn't noticed him before but perhaps being magic he could teleport from spot to spot. Weirder things had happened to me in the last few days. Or maybe not weirder things. Maybe I'd just become jaded to the whole idea of magic.

I felt as if I'd been overwhelmed with new ideas and new possibilities and couldn't conceive of their limits. Clearly, given how worn out I'd get doing magic, magic did have limits, but if I had more practice would those limits still remain? If the animals were, as Ian said, magic, did they have limits?

At any rate, the stallion walked slowly towards us. Socrates followed.

Ian waited. The calico paused to watch the stallion. He was majestic with his long legs and broad body. His eyes were as black as the rest of him. He looked more like a demon horse than a flesh and blood horse and yet, Ian assured me that he wasn't bad. Even the cats seemed respectful rather than fearful.

The calico sat and watched. Not an ear twitched.

When the stallion was closer, Socrates ran up to it and leaped, landing gently on the horse's back. I stood stunned. I had no idea what that meant.

The cat let out a loud meow and then leaped off.

"I guess that's an invitation," Ian said. He didn't sound particularly certain.

I'd never ridden a horse before. Most have weight limits that exclude me. It wasn't something that bothered me too much because while my sister adored horses and couldn't get enough, I'd never been bitten by the bug. Or maybe even as a child, I'd worried about being too heavy for a horse to carry.

The stallion snorted at me. And stomped a foot. Then he leaned down like a unicorn in front of a princess in a fairy tale.

"Really?" I asked. "Have you seen me?"

The horse stood up and took a good long look at me. His large nose nuzzled near my breast and then down the side of my body. He backed up and neighed in something like a shout of laughter.

Finally, he knelt back down on one front knee, something I didn't realize horses could do.

"I guess it's okay," Ian said. He seemed as uncertain as I did.

I walked over and rubbed the horse's back. It watched

me. I pushed myself up on his back. He didn't move. I swung a leg over.

I waited. The horse stayed in that position, now looking at Ian.

Ian sighed. He walked even more slowly than I had. He struggled a bit getting up on the horse, but finally made it.

"If we were in a movie, I'd be the sidekick who ends up sitting backwards," Ian said from behind me as the horse rose. "And then I'd be hanging onto the tail for dear life and everyone would be laughing at me even if it was a serious matter. Could you imagine the damage if we fell off?"

"You said the horse was the heart of the island. Do you really think he would let us fall off?" I asked.

"I can't believe he's letting us ride him," Ian said. "So far as I know, no one else has. At least not in anyone's memory."

The stallion walked, but his pace was far faster than mine would have been. Looking back at us and giving a snort, as if saying hang on, which I was doing, practically laying across his neck, the horse picked his pace up to a trot.

While he seemed to have no trouble with the pace, it felt impossibly fast to me, the ground seeming to race by at speeds I might go in a car. Wind whipped at my hair and face and only the body heat of the stallion kept me from shivering.

Ian hung onto me, squeezing me as tightly as I was squeezing the stallion. Neither of us were used to riding, so although, objectively, I knew the horse wasn't going that fast, it felt that way.

We raced across the island with no end in sight. The island felt larger than all of Lake Michigan, which, when I was a child, had seemed as large as an ocean. The horse topped a slight rise and then we were heading towards the back of Damien's home.

The windows had been smashed and the garden there trampled. I hadn't even noticed a garden but given the number of animals, I wasn't surprised that it was gone. From that vantage point, I could see the lake. And far on the horizon, I thought I saw a white speck that might have been a ferry. Or it could have been my imagination.

The stallion knelt and I slid off his back. Ian did the same. The calico cat, along with Socrates, appeared under the trampled and fallen bushes and followed us as we approached the house.

"I thought I saw the ferry approaching," I whispered to Ian. I had no idea why I was whispering.

"Me too," Ian said. "Which means we have maybe an hour to figure out what to do."

I sighed and looked at the cats.

"I don't suppose either of you have any ideas?"

The calico cat mewed at me and slipped through the broken glass of one of the French doors. She carefully avoided the shards that had broken, stepping neatly between them. I gave Ian a look and shrugged. We both followed her towards the door, but I paused when the knob didn't turn. Socrates brought up the rear, as if herding us towards a place only the cats understood.

I listened as Ian's feet still crunched against the broken glass. I hoped his shoes had solid soles. There were some large pieces around. I couldn't fit through the space the calico had used. I carefully reached through the empty frame of the French door and found a knob to unlock it and opened the door.

I heard the stallion snort as he moved off. I had no idea how far he went.

We were in a sun room with rust-colored tiles and plenty of windows, most of which had been broken. No blood stained the room so this hadn't been a fight. Perhaps the island was just angry with Damien.

An inner glass door was open and I walked into the kitchen. It had once been perfectly organized but someone or something had opened all the cabinets and pulled out everything. Pasta lay strewn across the floor, pots and pans had been pulled out and lay on their sides, at least one lid had rolled to a stop near a large kitchen island.

Shards of clay from once beautiful hand-done plates lay on the creamy tile floor in the kitchen. The room was open to the large room where Damien had brought me, with its large windows looking out over the lake.

Sharon sat calmly in a brown recliner style chair, the back near the solid wall of the fireplace.

"You," she said. "I should have known you'd be a problem the moment I laid eyes on you. And then Damien had to clean up your mess!"

Her voice was low but held an edge that I didn't think she was capable of.

"Sharon?" Ian asked, coming in. I glanced at him, the way his eyebrows pulled together. His face was pale.

Sharon smiled. "Ian. It was so good of you to tell me about Holly and help me find her."

I whirled.

Ian raised his hands and shook his head. "We always tell Sharon things. She's the mayor..." he choked back whatever else he was going to say.

"I should have listened to Damien when he told me this woman was a problem. Look at the island. We were peaceful and fine and then this woman came and the animals are all up in arms!" Sharon stood up, glaring at me, her eyes as hard as the stone I'd been sitting on for the last day or so.

"Damien started this," Ian said quietly. "Holly was related to Ann."

"Of course, Damien started this!" Sharon snapped. "He's ancient. He's the reason the island works the way it does!"

Ian said nothing.

"The island's magic comes from Damien?" I asked.

The calico cat growled softly from where it sat near my feet. It moved slightly in front of me, watching Sharon carefully.

My arms tingled and I raised my hands, hoping to protect myself. Something zinged and hit what seemed to be a large plastic wall in front of me, catching in it and then falling to the floor at the calico cat's feet.

"Damn Bernice!" Sharon snapped. "She's always teaching out of order."

"Is Damien the source of the island's magic?" I asked again.

"He's the reason we can tap it," Sharon said. "Because I've been a leader here, he's promised to show me his secret to immortality."

Which may have explained why this woman who had seemed so kind had been willing to follow Damien.

"You're really willing to sacrifice other people's lives for yours?" Ian whispered.

"A drowning man will fight for his life to keep his head above water," Sharon said. "It doesn't create an intent to kill."

"You're not drowning," Ian said.

"I had lung cancer that metastasized to my brain," Sharon said. "Five years ago. Right now, I'm pain free and, so far as I can tell, in remission. The doctors don't understand it. Even the ones here."

"Does that mean two bodies each year?" I asked.

"Aren't you the smart one," Sharon said, though it wasn't a question. It was the kind of snark I might expect from my ex-husband, not her.

I said nothing. It was always the best way to deal with my ex. Sharon was no different.

"Of course, that's what it means. My sacrifices started in April. I still have my connection to the island. It keeps me alive. And I'll protect Damien until he reconnects with the island himself," Sharon said.

I felt the hair on my arms raise. Not a tingle, so Sharon wasn't raising magic. But there was something going on. I stole a glance at Ian. He felt something to. He looked worried, which meant he didn't like what was happening.

I focused on my magic, lighting a fire in the fireplace, though it was across the room, behind Sharon.

Sharon jumped at the whoosh. She moved away from it, putting her back to the large windows. She glared at me.

"I'll stop your fire before it does any damage," she said. She closed her eyes.

I began to feel tired, as if someone was draining me. A chill stole over my body.

A gray cat appeared out of nowhere and leaped for Sharon's face. She twisted and ducked but I no longer felt quite as cold, though I did feel as if I'd run several miles in a race. Fatigued, but okay. I needed food and water. Ian's tea would help, too.

"I don't know why the island likes you so much," Sharon muttered. She kicked out at the gray cat which crouched down, just low enough and far enough away for Sharon's foot to miss. The sound of its hiss echoed in the room.

"Damien's first victim was an aunt of my mother's," I said. "She talked to the island about what he was doing. It knows."

"Damien controls the island!" Sharon snapped. "And he will again when he reconnects with it. I may not know how to manage it, but I can keep it from protecting you."

She threw fire at me. No shield stopped it, but the fire did no damage to me. Instead, it burned around me. The floor in the room was wood with a rug and that blackened from the flames. I felt as if I were sitting next to a fire warming myself.

The calico sat practically on my feet, watching me, eyes large.

The fire burned down more quickly than I'd have expected. Ian had stepped all the way back into the kitchen, where he leaned against the island, staring at me in horror.

"You're okay?" he whispered.

I nodded. Either my fire magic protected me or the island was doing it for me. I glanced down at the calico who had her head cocked and watched Sharon.

My arms barely started tingling when a torrent of water hit me. A small bubble formed around my face, just enough that I could breathe. I flailed around, trying to stand but the pressure was such that the water pushed me back towards the kitchen, until I hit a wall. Glass scraped at the back of my thighs as I tried to avoid falling.

I breathed too hard and too quickly in fear, despite the bubble. Seeing the water pouring at me, coming towards me created a primal terror of drowning. Then it, too, stopped.

My hands streamed with rivulets of blood from the glass that I'd been pushed against. The calico cat hadn't moved. Her fur was barely even damp and she flicked her head so that water droplets landed on the floor around her.

I waited for Sharon's next move. I wasn't so good with water, but I was decent with earth. Bernice had barely begun to teach me about air. I didn't know what I could do with spirit.

I closed my eyes, searching out anything that I could do with spirit. I didn't really know what I was doing. Just searching for anything that felt as if it were on my side.

Calm settled in my body as I felt things, everything from the trees and bushes, to the stones, and finally the magical creatures that looked like tiny flames in my mind's eye. I know I was connecting to them.

I asked for help, sending a wordless plea that held my confusion and fears and needs.

Moments later the room was filled with at least fifty people, none of whom looked quite solid, all of them looking at Sharon, ready to take her on.

Chapter Twenty-One

I hadn't thought that even Damien could have murdered this many people. They all stood around me in clothing from various ages. One man had a braided ponytail down his back and a tie-dyed t-shirt. Another woman had on loafers and cropped pants with a short bob held back by a large scarf. Still another woman wore a black floor-length dress from a long-ago era, her hair curled in ringlets.

"They aren't victims," Ann whispered to me. Her voice was more hollow than it had been and I could see the far wall through her. Her comment made me question who these people were, if not victims.

The calico cat stood up and arched her back into a stretch, watching. If cats could smile, she would have been.

Sharon pushed herself back into a corner.

A woman with auburn hair cut short in soft curls around the top of her head walked towards Sharon. I noted the polyester pants and the button-down blouse that appeared to have a print of small flowers on it. My grandmother had dressed like that in photos of my mother as a teenager.

"Sharon," the woman said. "Death is a part of life. To trade away your death for the deaths of others is to trade away life for an existence of sorrow and pain. It's not too late to give back."

"Bess Williamson?" Sharon's voice had a question in.

Bess nodded at her. I couldn't see the expression on her face.

"I'm not ready to die. It was happening too soon. Damien gave me a way out. He said the island approved! You know it never wants us to hurt!"

"It can't subvert the natural order. Damien managed to bastardize some spells and made a blood sacrifice of the one he thought he loved most to link himself to the power of the island. He has perverted the magic here. He needs to be stopped. As do you," Bess said.

Sharon shook her head.

I felt magic rising on my arms. Sharon tossed something into the ghosts. They disappeared for a moment. Sharon stood still, rigid. And then she relaxed, giving into a smile which she turned in my direction.

No sooner had she relaxed than the ghosts reappeared. They stood closer to her now than they had moments ago.

"I wouldn't do it," Bess said when Sharon raised her arms.

My own tingled but there was no release.

"Why not?" Sharon asked.

"We eat your power. You were linked to Damien's power. While you gained much, he still siphoned it off of you. That link isn't broken and through you he is still linked to the island," Bess said. "In our deaths, we are part of the island."

"I don't want to become part of the island!" Sharon snapped.

"Then it is best to die on the mainland, outside of our

enclaves. Your spirit will follow the path set for it during its transition. Each of us here has had a choice. You would still have a choice, though the island would demand reparation for what you have done."

Sharon shuddered. She looked around, her eyes rolling like a horse in a flaming barn. She was beyond terrified.

"I won't die here!" Sharon screamed. She pointed a finger into the center of the room.

Like always, my arms tingled, but this time my breath caught. I waited. My chest felt tight and it was hard to take in a deep breath.

Only then did I realize she was sucking the air out of the room. Just as I began to panic, Sharon released her spell. A huge funnel of wind swirled in the room, throwing small items around. The ghosts were sucked into the vortex. Next went the sofa. Sharon stood back from it.

I moved around the edge of the room until I was in the kitchen with Ian. The little calico followed me, watching.

Socrates let out a loud hiss but nothing changed. The ghosts didn't reappear. The air still swirled, picking up everything in the living room. The funnel didn't move so much as it grew wider.

"Maybe we should get out of here," I said to Ian. The noise from the funnel nearly drowned out my voice.

He looked at the cats who hadn't moved yet. He shook his head.

"They'll hold it where it is!" he called back. He pointed at Socrates and then the calico.

And so we waited. My arms were tingling so hard they began to throb and hurt. The funnel got smaller. The air seemed to fill with more oxygen, though I had been breathing just fine. And finally, the funnel wore itself out and the tingle on my arms stopped.

Sharon glared at us and started to head towards the front door. The calico leaped to stand in front of her.

I closed my eyes and sent a blast of fire to block the door. The calico moved out of the way. Sharon stopped in front of it. She tentatively reached out a hand, but quickly pulled it back.

I felt the warmth in my belly dissipating, my knees starting to tremble. I couldn't hold the fire for much longer.

Ian closed his eyes. My arms tingled. He raised clay bars up through the floor blocking the way. I let the fire drop. Sharon turned. She looked around. Ian and I stood between her and the kitchen. A hallway led around the front but I doubted there was an exit from there. She was trapped.

Sharon screamed.

The sound threatened to overwhelm my ears. I'd never heard anything that loud or that pained.

My arms tingled and the floor moved enough to throw me off balance. My knees hit the ground, the hard floor sending the agony of my cuts and bruises through my body. I groaned.

Fire hit me, but like the fire before, it danced around me and didn't actually burn. Sweat beaded on my forehead while I pushed myself up.

The calico cat leaped through the flames and cuddled on my lap, keeping me in a seated position.

"Send the flames back to their owner," a voice whispered. It couldn't possibly be the cat. but I had no idea who else it would be.

I closed my eyes, concentrating on sending the flames back. The air around me got cooler. The snap of the fire got quieter, but didn't go away.

Sharon screamed again, but this time it was definitely in pain.

My eyes snapped open.

The flames had gone back to their owner and Sharon's body was engulfed in them. I recoiled from the stink of burning flesh even as the screams died suddenly.

A blackened husk dropped to the ground and the flames died with it.

Silence echoed against the memory of the screams.

Only to be broken by more shrieks

Chapter Twenty-Two

I covered my ears against the sound that held both horror and sorrow. The pitch still reached me.

Hands reached for me and I looked up at Ian. He made a sound that I couldn't hear over the screaming. Except looking at him was enough to let me know the wails were coming from me.

"I killed her," I cried when he pulled me into a hug.

"You defended yourself," Ian said.

"I killed a woman! I killed *Sharon*." I could have lived with myself if it had been Damien. He'd looked the part of the villain the entire time. He'd acted even more like a villain. Sharon could have been my grandmother. And I'd killed her.

"You sent the flames back to her," Ian said. "It's a basic self-defense move. Most mages can catch their spells but Sharon wasn't expecting it from you. Granted, it's advanced for what you've been taught, but she should have reacted."

I sniffed. I wasn't sure it made me feel any better.

"We have to let Xavier know," I said. I could be arrested. I would probably be tossed off the island.

Socrates meowed, a loud yowl. His ears went flat as he looked at me.

"I don't think Socrates likes the idea," Ian said.

The calico cat remained with me. I rubbed her ears, letting the sound of a soft purr bring what comfort it could.

"Do you think Xavier is in on this?" I asked.

"I expect that while everyone knows that Damien isn't quite what he says and no one will act against him even as his spells fail, I'm not sure any of us knew about Sharon," Ian said. "That might take some explaining."

"I knew," Bernice said, walking into the room, looking around. She wrinkled her nose, probably the most expressive thing I'd seen her do the entire time I'd known her.

"Really?" Ian asked. "Or is this just more of your games about knowing things?"

"I felt her spells. I'm sensitive that way. It's why I'm the one who does the basic teaching. I can feel things like that. She was doing some sketchy stuff. Lots of power in here. I take it that was her?" Bernice pointed at the blackened husk that was once Sharon.

I nodded.

"Feels like a defense spell. You sent her flames back to her?" Bernice asked.

Another nod from me. My throat was tight and I didn't quite trust my voice any longer.

"A good mage would have caught them. Most mages wouldn't have been able to conjure enough power to destroy themselves like that, either. Not without help. And you aren't burned at all."

"I think the island is protecting Holly," Ian said.

"Could be. Could be. Family relationship to the ghost you were speaking to?" Bernice asked.

I nodded again. I had no idea how she knew all this.

"The enclaves have suspected something like this. I report to them on my annual travel," Bernice said. "Neil in California was the one who suggested I pay attention to Sharon. Everyone knew Damien was off, but it appears he was more off than anyone guessed."

Bernice glanced around the room again. "Where is he?"

"He left the island," Ian said. "I think he might be on his way back. He needs a human sacrifice to tie him back to the island's magic. It needs to be done on the full moon."

Bernice frowned. "I've never heard of such a thing. Neil was the most interested in what was going on here. Everyone felt the magic, but Neil and a couple of others said the magic didn't feel quite right, like it was muffled. I'm not sure anyone thought about human sacrifice. Or if they did, they weren't talking about it."

"I've heard that he learned it in a day," Ian said. "At least that's how the ghost who talked to Holly said it was done."

I cleared my throat before speaking. "He held onto Ann's hand and refused to let go when she got off the ferry. I guess he went through a day of training and then discovered that he could kill Ann and link to the island's magic. He didn't have any of his own, really."

"He must have stumbled upon the idea soon enough. The island wouldn't have been attached to Ann yet and as he didn't have magic, it wouldn't have seen him as much of a threat either. Clever of him."

Bernice took another look around the room, noted the cats with us and then began to walk around. Ian had let the bars descend back into the earth at some point. I'd not noticed, probably because I was so busy concentrating on sending fire back to Sharon and then on the fact that I'd murdered a woman.

"You aren't spelled by Damien?" Ian asked.

Bernice glanced over at him. "Eleanor cleared the linking spells on me about four years ago when I went to their enclave. They were light and intricate and if we hadn't been doing such deep personal work, no one would have noticed them. I'm sure her report was what interested Neil. He'd taken a dislike to Damien from the start, but couldn't quite put his finger on why."

"And Damien didn't notice?" I asked.

"I have my own spells," Bernice said. "You can learn a lot of things outside the island from other enclaves. They all have their ways of doing things."

"Are you going to help us take him down?" Ian asked. "Or are you here for yourself?"

His tone felt rude to me. I was willing to take whatever help we could get, no matter Bernice's reasons.

"Damien needs to be stopped. Immortality isn't part of the deal in magic. It goes against nature and, given that I taught you, you ought to know that magic is about the natural order." Bernice gave Ian a long hard look.

Ian looked uncomfortable and there was something about his stance that suggested he didn't quite trust Bernice's words. Neither Socrates nor the calico cat made any move towards her, but Socrates didn't immediately howl at her as if in contradiction, either. The island seemed to have a sense of who was safe and who wasn't, at least it did once taught, and the cats appeared to speak for it. Bernice wasn't there to hurt us, but the island wasn't sure about trusting her if the cats were any indication.

I continued to rub the calico's ears.

"Do you have a plan to take Damien down?" Bernice

asked as she moved through the wrecked living area. Her eyes took in the broken glass and china in the kitchen.

Ian shrugged.

"I could use some guidance," I said.

Socrates' ears perked up at that and the calico cat turned her head to watch Bernice.

"He's not linked to the island so he probably doesn't have much magic left…"

"He'll have reserves," Ian said. "It's not like the magic is stored elsewhere. He took it. It fills him."

"Then we have to get him to use up the magic," Bernice said. "He won't get more. If he can even use the magic he has. Expect that his spells could go awry."

She glanced at Sharon momentarily as if she were wondering if that's what had happened with Sharon. I followed her gaze, wondering the same thing. Maybe Sharon had tried to stop the flames but not being connected to the island she couldn't grasp that much magic when it was sent back to her.

Or not. Maybe a part of Sharon had listened to the words of her ghosts and didn't really have the stomach to kill people each and every year just to stay alive.

"We need a better place than this room," Bernice said. "He'll come in here but there aren't many ways to keep our backs to him. We need a place to face him with fewer doors."

Ian gestured and the door to the greenhouse from the kitchen sealed off and so did the door to the hallway.

"There. One door. Not many walls but the open area will let us fight as well as Damien. But if he comes in and it's too closed off, he might leave before we can stop him," Ian said.

"I'll leave blockading the main door to you once he comes in. Just change the layout like you did with the greenhouse so you don't have to hold something," Bernice said. "That will keep us all in here."

"We'll be just as trapped as he is," I pointed out.

"We have magic. And ours isn't just a reservoir that will run dry. Ours keeps growing. Just accept who you are and acknowledge those things that have shamed you and let the magic that comes from your own acceptance of yourself fill you," Bernice said.

Ian paced around the kitchen, the glass crunching beneath his feet. I hated the sound of it. My legs still felt weak. I was tired. I'd eaten but I'd also done a lot of magic. I wasn't sure I could do more.

"You're weak," Bernice said.

I nodded.

"Is there anything in the refrigerator that might help her?" Bernice asked Ian. "Something you can spell?"

Ian sighed as if being put upon but he went over there. No one or nothing had opened the doors earlier so hopefully the food in there would still be good.

While my sister's refrigerator might have overflowed with an assortment of foods, from fresh fruits and vegetables, to lunch meat and cheeses to an assortment of condiments and whatever leftovers she had packaged up, Damien's refrigerator looked like someone about to leave on a vacation for several months.

I noted ketchup and brown mustard in the door. He had a single apple in a bin. A sliver of a hunk of cheese remained in the deli section.

"Well that's just disappointing," Ian said. "Maybe we ought to offer cooking classes on the island so more people keep food?"

"I think most people like going into the grocery store about every day. It's a social thing," Bernice said.

Ian shrugged.

He looked in the freezer and found a bag of coffee tucked away. Grinning he searched around for a coffee maker. That, unfortunately was on the floor, smashed.

"Well, it was a thought."

Bernice frowned. "I'll run and get some food. Hopefully, I'll be fast enough." She hurried out, not running but moving quickly as she always did, her back so straight she might have been required to carry a book on her head.

"Now what?" I asked Ian.

He came and sat down next to me, crossing his legs easily. Socrates waited with him. The calico cuddled on my lap.

"I guess we wait for Damien."

"How can we be sure he'll come here?" I worried he'd take someone off the ferry and bring her to the cavern system or some other place I hadn't yet seen. I couldn't imagine coming back to this mess.

"The island led us here," Ian said. "And the cats aren't going anywhere else, so for the moment, he's probably heading this way. Or else there's something here we need to do."

"I thought I saw a ferry on the horizon when we got here. It seems like he should be here now, if he were coming," I said.

Socrates stretched and headed out towards the front door. The calico stood up and looked back at me before starting to follow him. Ian helped me up and we hurried through the living room to the front door.

The sky was pink on the horizon, the sun setting quickly. Socrates hurried down the steps. The calico waited for us before following him. I looked back at Ian who shook his head but started to move. I wrapped the blanket closer around me and went last.

We were barely at the bottom of the stairs, my legs

feeling weak from the magic I'd done earlier, my stomach growling, when I heard a small hum that got louder.

"Golf cart," Ian said. The cats sat waiting, muscles tense.

In books or movies, a villain would show up on a giant horse or a high-powered SUV. Here, Damien arrived in a golf cart, a girl sitting next to him looking half-asleep. She appeared drugged, but it could have been a spell, though I had a feeling he wouldn't waste magic if he could use something mundane, not now.

Bernice was nowhere to be seen.

"Don't expect help. Bernice was no match for me," Damien said, looking down his nose at us.

"The island wouldn't let you kill her," Ian said.

Damien smiled. "No, sadly. I'll have to take her off island to do that, but sleep isn't a bad thing, is it?"

He didn't even twitch a finger but I felt the magical energy in the tingle of my arms. Like a wind, it flew towards us. Ian or one of the cats put up a shield. The wind that reached us moved around us and into the woods.

Damien's eyes narrowed. He said nothing.

Another tingle and something else flew at us. Another shield. This time Ian had a hand up. When the magic hit, I watched him stagger.

Damien wasn't using elements like Sharon. He had other magic.

He raised his left hand and threw something magical at us but it crashed into the shield leaving us temporarily blinded by something black and oily.

The shield dropped for a moment, just as a knife came flying through the air. Ian didn't have time to get another magical shield up, so we each dived to one side as the knife turned end over end to hit the stairs behind me.

Another knife was already flying towards me but at the

last minute it veered off course as if hit by a strong wind and landed point down in the ground.

I crawled over to grab it.

Damien stood in front of the golf cart. I couldn't risk throwing the knife at him with the girl in the seat. She wasn't attached to the island so I couldn't risk hurting her. Damien wasn't throwing spells that I could send back to him. I had no idea if the island would allow the knife to hit him or not.

Ian threw a fire spell at Damien, who countered it easily by sending it back to Ian who caught the magic easily. The fire had looked like a red baseball and Ian caught in one hand bringing his other hand over it, smothering the magic.

For an instant Ian's arms glowed faintly red before going back to normal.

I crawled around to the side while Damien concentrated on Ian. I stopped when Damien's gaze flicked to me. The calico cat stayed with me. Socrates stayed near Ian.

"If you can hear me, the girl is a human being and she shouldn't be hurt," I told the cat.

The calico flicked her ears at me.

"I would be hurt if she's hurt," I said quietly.

Damien threw a spell of long ropes to wrap themselves around me. I tried to think of a way to block them but the other protective spells had not been my own. It was too late to send the spell back to the sender by the time I realized I had no idea what I was doing.

Ropes wrapped themselves around me. They began to squeeze.

I panted, struggling to get a breath. The squeezing eased though the ropes remained around my body. Apparently, the island would only do so much to help us. Or else it didn't understand that not being able to move our arms and legs would be a problem.

I mean, it was a hunk of rock with trees and houses growing on it. No doubt it didn't have a clue about the importance of movement. Of course, if the island was magic, like the cats, you'd think that it would get that.

Damien smirked and threw the same spell towards Ian, who countered it with a send back spell. He was fast.

I concentrated on a tiny flame at the edge of the rope, not enough to burn me but enough to burn through the ropes. If I did it wrong, I was counting on the island to save me.

Fear raced up my spine as the warmth gathered in my belly. I sent out what I thought of as a tiny puff, a mere drop of flame and small flame, a spark, really centered on the ropes. They began to smoke.

The ground thundered beneath me. I looked up, expecting to see Damien having created an earthquake.

Instead, a large tree had fallen across the entrance to his house. Ian's leg was trapped under one of the branches and he was trying to move.

Damien faced him, walking just a little closer.

Socrates leaped from the tree and into Damien's face.

I heard the cat scream.

I looked up in time to see Damien toss Socrates to one side. The black cat landed on his feet, glaring at his opponent. Damien ignored the cat and turned back to Ian.

The ropes around me loosened and I pushed myself free from them. The calico looked at me with the sort of looks that cats give when you've offered them a particularly tasty treat.

I had dropped the knife when the ropes wrapped around me. Not that it would have helped when they had me tied up. I hadn't been able to move a finger.

I scooped it up.

Damien had his side to me. The girl in the cart was well behind him. Even if I missed Damien, I wouldn't hit her.

"Please let me hit him," I whispered.

I felt the weight of the knife in my hand. My axe throwing experience came back to me. I hoped it hadn't just been pure luck.

I breathed in and out slowly, getting ready. I nudged my magic, hoping that there was something that would let the knife fly true.

I tossed it away, overhand, watching as it spun end over end.

I watched as it appeared it would hit Damien in the neck, a perfect throw.

Instead, at the last minute it dropped and hit him in the upper arm.

While it didn't kill him, it stuck his flesh. He grimaced in pain or perhaps annoyance. Turning to his arm, he grabbed it. Then he turned back to me, leaving Ian alone for the moment.

I raised more warm energy, thinking about sleep. He'd claimed to have done that to Bernice. I pictured sleeping medication flowing into his veins and let the warmth go.

Damien was too busy trying to staunch the flow of blood from his arm to notice the spell. In less than a breath, he slumped over, asleep.

Ian still wiggled beneath the tree.

I took a step over to help him, but my legs buckled. I'd never felt so weak in my life.

I pulled myself closer to him, hoping to rescue him before Damien came around.

The calico cat walked next to me, keeping an eye on Damien. Socrates marched over to him and sat on him, his face in Damien's face. I had no doubt that he would attack the moment Damien made any sort of move.

The earlier wounds on my legs and knees throbbed and ached as I crawled towards Ian. I left a thin trail of blood.

The tree blocked my way. I needed to climb over it but wasn't sure I had it in me. I was halfway over it when Bernice stumbled towards us.

"Shit," she mumbled. She shook her head and walked at a normal human pace, probably half of her regular pace to the tree and easily climbed over it. She stifled a yawn as she knelt down by Ian.

My arms started to tingle. The tree raised enough for Ian to pull his leg from beneath it.

When he was clear, Bernice let it fall and looked back at Damien.

"I suppose the island wouldn't let you kill him?" she said.

I shook my head.

"Damn." She stared at him for a long moment. I felt my arms tingle again. I yawned.

"A nice deep sleep spell. Yours was good but not as deep as mine. He needs to stay there until I can get help," Bernice said. She glanced at the house and back the way she came. She sighed and climbed over the tree before heading up the stairs.

I was too tired to wonder what she was doing. It occurred to me after a bit that she could easily be just as bad as Damien. Maybe he had something she wanted there and would come back down and destroy us after she had it. Or, like Damien, maybe she had to keep us on her side for a time before linking to the island. Immortality had to be tempting for anyone.

Damien was stirring. Ian spelled him to keep him from waking up.

The girl in the cart woke up, shaking her head.

"You're going to be okay," I said.

She started and stared over at me. The day was gone and the sky was navy and dotted with clouds. I shivered where I sat. The blanket wasn't nearly warm enough. The chill from the ground had seeped up into my bones and I didn't know if I'd ever get warm again. The calico had curled up underneath the blanket and purred at me, so at least my lap was warm.

Ian didn't look much better despite having a heavier jacket. It had been ripped and torn in the battle with Damien.

The girl didn't say anything to me. She sat frozen on the seat of the golf cart.

"I don't have it in me to put her to sleep," Ian said. "I'm not sure I could spell food to wake myself up much less you."

"What can Bernice be doing in there?" I asked.

Just as the words came from my mouth, Bernice stepped down the stairs. "Looking for a phone," she said. "Xavier is on his way, along with Carl and the doctor."

I felt a tingle on my arms and the girl in the golf cart slumped into sleep.

"Will he believe us?" I asked.

"You didn't kill anyone," Bernice said.

I started to speak.

"If someone sends a spell back, that's not considered murder," Bernice said. "I suppose there might be some convoluted way to make it into murder, but you don't have the skill to have done anything like that. Xavier will look at the facts and arrest Damien."

"He can get out, though," I said. "I mean magic?" I had no idea how arresting someone would work on the island.

"There are ways to keep people from being able to utilize their magic. It's not like we're crime free," Bernice said. "Being a mage doesn't mean everyone is nice and kind, although we have such a small population, we don't have very much crime."

I heard the putt and chug of a small engine. Xavier came around the corner in a golf cart. The big man, Carl was next to him, his head ducked and back slumped to fit inside the little cart. Even Xavier's head nearly brushed the top. Carl was out and spelling Damien before the cart came to a complete stop.

Xavier walked over to Ian and looked him up and down. Then he looked at me. He closed his eyes slightly and nodded.

"What happened?" he asked, including both of us in his question.

Ian started talking first and I let him. I was too tired to tell everything that happened. In fact, when I heard another hum of a small machine, I let my eyes close and drifted off to sleep.

Chapter Twenty-Three

I woke up in a hospital setting—cream walls and the stink of chemical cleaners and medications. An IV was attached to my arm and I was covered with a thick blanket. The calico cat snoozed on my belly, which surprised me. Most hospitals wouldn't allow that. Of course, it was probably hard to stop a magic cat.

The blanket was cream like the walls. Pale gray blinds covered a window to the outside. The lights were off and I had no idea whether it was still night or daytime. I would have thought that someone could have given me something to perk me up at Damien's but apparently not.

This sent me into a flurry of worry that I'd somehow hit my head somewhere and I'd dreamed the whole Jewel Island thing. I didn't want the island to be a dream. I frantically searched the walls looking for anything that might tell me where I was.

My heart rate spiked as fear slinked through my body. I felt a light sweat on my arms. The calico raised her head. Of course. No real hospital would have a cat. I was foolish to forget that. The calico tugged at the blanket so she could get under it and snuggle even closer. I relaxed into the feeling of her purr.

I let myself doze back off, but the moment someone came in the room, my eyes snapped open.

"It's about time you woke up," Carl said. He pulled up a stool. Even sitting he was tall enough that he rather loomed over the bed.

"I would have thought they'd give me something for overdoing it," I said.

"They did." Carl gave me a gentle smile. "You were also somewhat hypothermic so they brought you here for some good old-fashioned medicine rather than just spells. Bodies need that, too."

I smiled a little. Now that he mentioned it, I was thirsty. Carl got up and went out, returning with a cup and a pitcher of water. After pouring the water carefully into the plastic cup, he handed it to me.

I drank deeply, but tried to be mindful that I hadn't had much in the last few days.

"How long have I been here?" I asked when I'd finished.

"Almost twenty-four hours," Carl said. "Xavier will be in shortly to get your statement, if you're up to it. I gave him a ring when I got your water."

I thought about what had happened, wondering how much Xavier and Carl already knew.

"Did Ian tell you everything?" I asked.

"Everything he knew," Carl said gently. "As did Bernice. There are a few people around who are upset that we've arrested Damien. Despite not having his own magic, the spells he wove are strong."

"What does that mean for me?" I asked.

"I wouldn't eat anything that Ian doesn't serve at the

B&B," Carl replied. I would have laughed but he looked serious.

"Darla wouldn't do that would she?" I asked.

"The island wouldn't let her if it understood." Carl gave the calico that peeked her head out from under the blanket a long look. In fact, he stared at her so long it began to make me uncomfortable.

I fidgeted a bit and found the button to raise the head of the bed a bit more so that I was more even with Carl's face. I'd been sleeping practically sitting up, but now I was fully upright.

His face remained serious as he talked about Darla.

"Has she said anything about Damien's arrest?" I asked.

"She's screaming that he didn't do anything." Carl clearly wanted to say more but then stopped himself.

I sighed.

I asked a few more questions while I waited for Xavier. It wasn't long before he arrived and took my story. Carl left us alone.

I started from where Damien had put a spell on me to force me to follow him to his house. I talked about the animals coming to the rescue. Then about following the calico cat into a tree on the island and then the cave, where I destroyed Ann's skeleton. Finally, I talked about Socrates leading Ian to me in the cave and how we left to find Damien.

Xavier made notes on a pad. I would have thought magic would allow him to remember things but perhaps it didn't quite work that way.

I cried when I talked about Sharon.

"You merely sent the spell back to her," Xavier said. "She started the murderous flames, not you. It's her own doing."

"I really liked her," I said in a small voice.

"We all did. But that doesn't mean she didn't do something horribly wrong. Even if you hadn't been able to send the spell back to her, it's clear the island was bonded enough to you to keep her from murdering you. All that would have happened is that you'd have been even more tired by the time Damien arrived and had two people to fend off. If Damien had killed that poor young girl, he would have linked to the island and possibly been able to subvert the no-killing rule."

I shuddered at the thought.

"Even if he hadn't, you used far more magic than your body knew how to handle. Basically, you exhausted yourself. The island likely wouldn't have saved you from that exhaustion, figuring you knew what you were doing."

The calico cat perked its head up and looked over at Xavier as if questioning his suggestion.

Xavier led me through the rest of my story right up to the point that he arrived.

"From the point you met up with Ian, your stories match. I suspect Damien will be hard pressed to find an attorney willing to take his case."

"Does he get tried here on the island or somewhere else?" I asked.

"He'll be tried at another enclave. I think Arizona wants him, but they have been investigating him for years so a good attorney can argue bias and get him sent elsewhere."

"How can there be an enclave in Arizona if the enclaves are on islands?" I asked. I was feeling tired. And hungry. I'd finished all the water in the pitcher and my body was starting to ache for something more.

"Not all enclaves are on islands. They work well for us because we can remain isolated but some, like the one in

Arizona, are up in the hills. There's one in Kentucky that works like that as well," Xavier said. "Now, you need to eat and to rest some more. Bernice will probably be back later to answer more questions."

No sooner had Xavier left than someone brought in a huge tray with plenty of food. I had been expecting a tray of mystery meat under gravy and perhaps some fruity gelatin, but the food on this tray could have been from a five star restaurant.

The woman carrying it, dressed in scrubs, had to be a nurse. "Don't look so shocked. In cases like yours, Derry's delivers."

I noted her name badge said Cassandra.

"Thank you," I told her. "This is huge." I noted slices of roast chicken, a baked potato, roasted Brussel sprouts, thick bread and butter, some sort of pasta salad that appeared to have meat, small appetizer rolls with an assortment of deli meats and vegetables on them. In addition, I noticed a large mug of what looked like the tea that Ian served me.

"Don't worry. I expect that as tired as you were, you'll eat most of it," Cassandra said. She was tall and slim with brilliant red hair kept in a long braid.

"Do you get much business here?" I asked. I still wanted to know more about the island.

"Lots of accidents," Cassandra said. "Dr. Mulrooney and I both have healing magic so we can work on the physical or magical level. The accidents might be magical but the bodily injuries are often physical, so that's important. And we have general wellness stuff to attend to."

We made small talk for some time. I was mostly done with dinner when Cassandra stood up. "I think you have an admirer here," she said.

I half expected David to show up and was surprised

when Carl walked into the room just after Cassandra left. I felt my cheeks warm. He was a nice looking man and plenty large enough that I wasn't going to go through the fears that I was too big for him or worrying about hurting him with my size. In college, I'd dated a very thin computer nerd and I was always worried that I would crush when he'd pull me on top of him. It didn't help that he'd groan and hiss that I had to get off because I was killing him.

"I see they got around to feeding you," Carl said.

I felt foolish eating something. I'd hardly talked to Carl before this, only when he'd sat by my bed. I found it hard to believe he was an admirer.

"They did," I said, sipping at the tea, which perked me up more than all the food. I'd even eaten a brownie, though I still had bread and butter and a bit of cheese left.

"I exhausted my magic once chasing a guy who had a thing for earrings. Ultimately stealing earrings was sort of his power so he'd completely accepted that's what he did and he kept throwing spells at me while I tried to bring him in. He got away for a few days, but Xavier caught him while I was still resting up," Carl laughed a bit.

"Whatever happened to the girl Damien brought here?" I asked.

"Rose, who you probably met at the front desk in the department, took her on the ferry and said she found her wandering. If the girl says anything, no one will believe her or else think someone gave her something to make her hallucinate," Carl said. "Security made sure her family was notified. College student."

I was glad she'd be okay.

Bernice walked in, her pace, as always, faster than anyone else's. Carl stood up, ready to move.

"Have a seat," Bernice said. "I'm just here to answer

questions and you probably know some specifics I don't. I haven't exactly been briefed."

Carl pulled at the front legs of his pants before he sat back down. Bernice grabbed another chair from a corner and pulled it up to the other side of the bed.

"How is Ian?" I asked. I'd tried to remember to ask about him a dozen or more times but something else always came up in conversation.

"He and Socrates are fine," Bernice said. "He's back at the B&B. Darla wasn't pleased and made her displeasure known. The B&B is Ian's. He's bonded to that building like a lover, so Darla's now looking for employment. They don't trust her at Derry's so I'm not sure what she'll do."

I glanced at Carl and he smiled. "Ian just got back this morning."

Clearly there were things he hadn't known.

"What happens if she can't find a job?" I asked.

"She has bills like everyone else, and while she'll have a stipend, it's not likely to be enough for her," Bernice said. "The island takes care of us, but not that well. She can apply off-island or at another enclave. They won't take her wherever they hold Damien, though. I expect she'll have to leave as she's always done hospitality work. The enclave near New Orleans would be good for her, but I doubt she has the stomach for it."

"Who's going to be the next mayor?" I asked.

"I am," Bernice said. "I think it's time I took more responsibility on the island. I have a feeling there's a new teacher about to show up soon enough and I can let teaching go. Ever since I sent Damien into a slumber, I've been more aware of the island and its workings, even more than before."

"You mean there's no election?" I asked.

"Every fourth year," Carl said. "This is interim, so the

island and the council can appoint her. Sharon had two more years on her latest term, so Bernice has two years to make herself more likable, or at least do enough that people respect her job."

I smiled. Bernice didn't much care what people thought of her but I had a feeling she'd be a great mayor.

"How come I didn't get a party like this?" Ian asked. He carried balloons as he sashayed in, looking none the worse for wear.

"What about your leg?" I asked.

"Lots of cuts and bruises and scrapes, but there are some magical potions around here that keep me from feeling it. Mostly." He frowned at the thought. "I was lucky. A few more inches and it wouldn't have been a branch holding me down but the whole tree. Cassandra said I could have lost the leg had that happened."

"Everyone out," a woman said. Her dark hair was pulled back tightly around her head and she looked at me. "I'm Dr. Mulrooney. It's nice to finally get to meet you."

"Nice to meet you," I said.

Dr. Mulrooney looked at the others, giving them each a glare as they moved out of the room.

"Don't tell Ian but if Socrates hadn't been there and decided to heal him, he'd have been on crutches for months." She took out a stethoscope and started listing to my lungs and heart, with barely a pause.

I breathed in and out when she told me and let her check the bandages on my legs. The calico cat stretched and watched.

"You're going to have find a name for her soon enough," Dr. Mulrooney said.

I hadn't even thought about that, though I had wondered what I ought to call the little calico.

"Me?" I asked.

"She seems to have adopted you. Consider it an honor. Lots of people never get adopted by one of the island cats. I keep hoping for that stallion, but that's me, unrequited love. Of course, me and half the island," Dr. Mulrooney said as she nodded.

"I think another night and you'll be good to go. That tea perking you up?"

"It is," I said.

"Good. You'll get real rest then instead of just your exhausted rest. Helps you heal better. Cassandra will change the bandages once more. We removed plenty of debris from a few of those cuts while you were out but I don't expect you'll have any lasting damage."

The doctor turned to leave. "It was nice meeting you. Too bad it was under these circumstances."

I nodded and waved a little.

The room felt too quiet now that everyone was gone.

Ann Rodgers appeared near the bed. She was barely an outline this time, but I still recognized her. "Thank you. All of us are free now that Damien has been cut off from the island magic. When I was a girl, I had a calico cat named Peony."

As Ann faded out, I looked at the little calico. "Do you want to be Peony?" I asked.

She gave a small mew. I nodded at her. So that was settled. I leaned back to get a bit more sleep. I'd had a busy few days and I needed it.

About Bonnie Elizabeth

Bonnie Elizabeth could never decide what to do, so she wrote stories about amazing things and sometimes she even finished them.

While rejection stung her so badly in person, she spent most of her young life talking to cats and dogs rather than people, she was unusually resilient when it came to rejections on her writing, racking up a good number of them.

Floating through a variety of jobs, including veterinary receptionist, cemetery administrator, and finally acupuncturist, she continued to write stories.

When the internet came along (yes she's old), she started blogging as her cat, because we all know cats don't notice rejection. Then she started publishing.

Bonnie writes in a variety of genres. Her popular Whisper series is contemporary fantasy and her Teenage Fairy Godmother series is written for teens. She has been published in a number of anthologies and is working on expanding her writing repertoire.

She lives with her husband (who talks less than she does) and her three cats, who always talk back.

Find her at www.bonnielizabeth.com

Stay in Touch

f

Also by Bonnie Elizabeth

The Frost Witch Saga

October Snow

November Frost

December Storm

Familiar Cafe Series

Unfamiliar Magic

Unfair Magic

Appalachian Souls

Souls Lost

Souls Broken

The Ash Jericho Series

An Inheritance to Die For

A Discovery to Die For

A Distraction to Die For

The Whisper Novels

Whisper Bound

Taken by the Sound

An Air of Suspicion

Little Dog Lost

Death Interrupted

Down in Whisper

A Haunting Whisper

A Haunting Attraction

Secrets Not Whispers

Only Human

Other Novels

One Bad Wish

Sun Spot Magic

Ghosts from the Past

Unnatural Secrets

Shadows of Solstice

The Haunting of Steely Woods

Find them all at your favorite bookseller or check us out at
MyBigFatOrangeCat.com